gh

D0333130

Megan Sparks
Roller Girls

Books in the
Roller Girls series

Falling Hard
Hell's Belles
In a Jam
Boot Camp Blues

Megan Sparks

Roller Girls

Hell's Belles

With special thanks to Lisa Fiedler

First published in 2013 by Curious Fox,
an imprint of Capstone Global Library Limited,
7 Pilgrim Street, London, EC4V 6LB
Registered company number: 6695582

www.curious-fox.com

Text © Hothouse Fiction Ltd 2013

Series created by Hothouse Fiction
www.hothousefiction.com

The author's moral rights are hereby asserted.

Cover designed by Jo Hinton-Malivoire, original concept by
www.spikyshooz.com
Illustrations by Allan Campbell

ISBN 978 1 78202 033 2

1 3 5 7 9 10 8 6 4 2

A CIP catalogue for this book is available from the British Library.

Typeset in Baskerville by Hothouse Fiction Ltd

Printed and bound by CPI Group (UK) Ltd, Croydon, CRO 4YY

For Shannon and Ricky, who skate on blades,
not wheels. Thanks for being my team!

Chapter One

$3x - 7 = 2x - 2$ Solve for x.

Annie sighed. She had no idea how to solve for x, but there was a lemon tart in the display case that would help solve the growling in her stomach.

She swept her long brown hair into a messy bun, closed her maths book and thought up her own equation: Annie + a steaming cup of chamomile tea = heaven.

Pushing aside her homework, she rose and crossed the black and white checkerboard floor of Rosie Lee's, the café she and her dad had recently opened in his hometown of Liberty Heights, Illinois. It was hard to believe that a few short weeks ago, the shop had been filthy and covered in cobwebs. A lot of hard work had gone into transforming it into the cosy place it was now, but it had been a labour of love – the shop was Dad's dream.

Although from the frown on his face as he bent over the spreadsheets arranged on the counter, the dream looked like it had become a nightmare. Annie guessed that he was having some maths trouble too.

"I must take after you," Annie joked, reaching into the case and removing the cream-topped pastry. "No head for numbers."

"You can say that again," Dad grumbled. He dropped his pencil and ran a hand through his brown hair. "I can measure out baking powder with the best of them and calculate the proportion of butter to flour with my eyes closed. It's subtracting monthly expenses from income that trips me up."

Annie glanced around the empty shop and grimaced. Things had got off to a good start, but lately the only foot traffic in and out of the shop consisted of people popping in to hang notices on the "community bulletin board" Dad had installed. The people had been grateful for the advertising space, but once they'd pinned their flyers to the corkboard, they'd hurried off to finish distributing their materials. The guy who'd posted an index card advertising a "2003 Toyota Camry with low mileage" had bought himself a small coffee to go, but other than that, none of the bulletin board people had purchased a thing.

"So has there been any?" Annie asked. "Income, I mean."

Dad hesitated, as though he might be about to fib. Then he showed her the number on the calculator screen. "Not much, Beanie."

Annie rolled her eyes at the use of his nickname for her.

Beanie was short for "String Bean", which referred to Annie's long, lanky frame. She'd shot up nearly a foot last year which had sadly put a swift end to her gymnastics career. On the upside, she now had the tall, slender figure of a model. She really didn't mind the Beanie thing. It was so Dad – cute and a little bit silly.

What wasn't silly was the money issue. Nothing cute about "not much income". Annie had been afraid that would be the case. When they'd opened the British eatery they'd both had high hopes. Dad's baking was superior and the space was warm and welcoming. It had seemed like a no-brainer to Annie – they were going to be a big hit. But here it was, four weeks later on a crisp, early autumn afternoon; customers should have been flocking in for hot tea and cinnamon scones warm from the oven. Instead, the cheery little place was utterly deserted.

As though he were reading her mind, Dad motioned to the empty tables. "I must be doing something wrong, but for the life of me, Annie, I can't imagine what it is."

His voice was a mixture of confusion and disappointment. It made Annie's heart sink.

"Don't say that, Dad," she said, placing the tart on the counter and throwing her arms around him. "You're doing everything right. The food is brilliant, the shop is the cutest place in town, and ... and..." Unfortunately, she didn't have a third "and" to add, so she just hugged him tighter. "It'll be fine. It takes time for a place like Rosie Lee's to catch on. But once it does, we'll have customers queuing round the block."

Dad pressed a kiss to Annie's forehead and chuckled. "Now

I remember why I dragged you here all the way from London. To be my own personal cheerleader."

Annie winced. Sore subject. She'd been chosen for the Liberty Heights High School cheerleading squad, but had had the audacity to turn them down. That decision had pretty much made her Public Enemy Number One in the eyes of Kelsey Howard, the most popular girl in school. Instead of picking up a pair of pom-poms, she'd stepped into a pair of roller skates and joined Liberty Heights' junior roller derby league.

And derby girls, it seemed, were always hungry.

Tummy grumbling, she picked up the lemon tart, then pointed to a gorgeous chocolate-frosted cake under a glass dome on top of the display case.

"Gather your rations, sailor," she commanded, doing her best Navy Admiral impersonation. "Then muster at our usual table."

"Aye, aye, captain," said Dad, snapping her a silly salute. He punched the off button on his calculator and grabbed a knife.

Moments later they were seated by the large window, bent over their desserts. Annie tasted Dad's cake – it was beyond delicious. And the buttery crust of her lemon tart was so delicate that it actually melted in her mouth. If only people would try Rosie Lee's, she was certain it would become their favourite place in the world.

"You really outdid yourself with this batch," she told her father, using her baby finger to mop up a smear of lemon filling from her plate. "Who cares if you're hopeless with numbers and spreadsheets. You're an absolute wizard in the kitchen."

Dad gave her a grateful smile. "I appreciate the rave review, Beanie, but the fact remains: we need customers if we're going to stay afloat." He put down his fork and stared at the mural on the wall behind Annie. It was a red double-decker London bus filled with remarkably lifelike portraits of some of Britain's most celebrated citizens. And the best part was that it was custom-designed and hand-painted by Annie's best friend, Lexie.

But Annie could see from the look on Dad's face that he was suddenly missing one British citizen in particular. "If your mum were here she'd certainly get our financials in order," he said softly.

"Maybe." Annie frowned. "But she's *not* here."

After her parents separated, Annie's American-born Dad had decided to leave England and return to the United States. Annie had been given the choice to remain in London with Mum, or try life in America with Dad. It had been the most difficult decision of her life, but ultimately she'd chosen to go with Dad. Throughout Annie's whole life, it was always Dad who had really been there for her. Mum loved Annie and Annie loved her, but she was always busy at her law firm.

The truth was, Annie missed her mother a lot, but this wasn't the time to wallow in that. Dad needed to get his confidence back and thinking about his failed marriage and his ex-wife, thousands of miles away across the ocean, probably wasn't the way to do it.

On the other hand, Annie felt a little tingle of hope. If Dad missed Mum – and maybe not just for her business skills – that could mean there was a chance they'd consider trying again.

Of course, that would require Mum taking her nose out of her law books and legal briefs long enough to miss him, too.

Dad was still looking wistfully at the mural. "It was a gamble, taking you away from all your friends and bringing you to America. I hope I didn't make a mistake."

"You didn't," Annie assured him. "Going to an American high school is amazing. It's like being in a teen drama! Honestly, sometimes I think I'm going to walk into the cafeteria and see the cast of *Glee* or *90210*. It's been really fun."

"Good – as long as you don't turn into a drama queen yourself!" Dad joked.

Annie had enough real-life, Liberty Heights High drama queens to deal with already. But she didn't mention that to her father.

"And you didn't *take* me," she reminded him, slapping her hand on the white tablecloth. "I chose to come. And here I am. So let's not be gloomy about it. Let's figure out a way to make it work!"

Dad sat back in the chair and blinked at her. Annie knew he was surprised by her assertiveness. Frankly, so was she. The old Annie had been more quiet and reserved, and a lot less confident. The old Annie might have turned and ran the minute the cheerleader captain, Kelsey, looked at her sideways. The old Annie probably would have already accepted defeat and begun packing her bags to head back across the ocean to London.

But the old Annie wasn't a roller girl!

Annie popped up from her chair and put one hand on her hip,

affecting the persona of a cranky, wise-cracking diner waitress.

"You done here, pal? We got other customers waitin' for this table, ya know. Meatloaf's the blue plate special tonight. Can't keep them regulars away when that one's on the menu." She chomped on her imaginary chewing gum. "So you ready to pay, or what?"

Dad faked a frown. "Well, since I know the chef personally, I thought this might be on the house."

"Oh, fine." Annie rolled her eyes and pretended to fluff her imaginary beehive hairdo. "Just be sure you leave a decent tip. You think I woik my tail off in this joint for the fun of it?"

Dad quickly reached into his pocket and pulled out a couple of notes.

"Jeesh," she huffed, sweeping up the bills from the tabletop and tucking them into the neckline of her shirt. "Two whole bucks. Ain't that generous? I'll try not to spend it all in one place!"

With a clatter, she gathered the plates and cutlery from the table, balanced them on her palm and held them high above her head as she sashayed off towards the kitchen. She could hear Dad's laughter following her all the way to the sink.

Annie was pleased at having made Dad laugh. He needed some distraction from all the pressure. As she ran hot water over the smudges on the plate and brushed the crumbs of tart crust into the drain, she thought about the two dollars Dad had "tipped" her. It gave her an idea.

Why couldn't she *really* bring in a little extra money? She was fourteen years old, after all. She should be contributing. And not just by working for free at Rosie Lee's – by actually earning some extra cash.

So what could she do? Between school, homework, and her roller derby practice schedule, she'd need extremely flexible hours. And she knew that here, anyone under sixteen wasn't allowed to work at night during the school year. This was going to take some serious thought.

She dried her hands on a paper towel and returned to the cosy little dining area where Dad had gone back to his invoices and bank statements. He was attacking his paperwork with new resolve and she didn't want to bother him. So she went back to the table where she'd left her algebra homework and sat down.

But she couldn't concentrate on her assignment.

She had to find a way to earn some extra money until the shop got off the ground.

She thought about applying for a job in one of the cool clothing stores at the mall, but there were two problems with that: one, Dad would be too busy to drive her, and two, she'd probably spend ninety per cent of her pay buying clothes with the employee discount.

Frustrated, she tapped her pencil on her notebook, and stared out of the window.

A young woman was approaching along the pavement. Annie noted absently that she was pushing a buggy – no, wait, this was America, so it was a stroller – and appeared to be completely exhausted. One glance in the stroller and Annie understood why: triplets!

Annie watched her pause outside the door to Rosie Lee's. Annie guessed that she was debating with herself about coming in, telling herself she should really get home and get dinner started. But if ever there was a person who needed a good cup of tea, it was her!

Annie sprang up from her chair and flew to the door, opening it with a big smile.

"Hello, there," she said, turning on the charm of her British accent. "Can I give you a hand?" She held the door open as far as it would go to accommodate the giant stroller and beamed at the three babies in the seats. "Oh, look at them! They're gorgeous!"

And they were. The chill in the afternoon air had given their plump little cheeks a rosy glow. There was very little hair on their heads, but based on the colours of their outfits, Annie was able to surmise that there were two boys and one girl. She pointed to the pale pink wool of the baby girl's jumper and beamed. "We have cupcakes iced in that exact colour!"

If the triplets' mother had been considering going on her way, it was clear that she was now seriously entertaining the idea of stopping in. Annie guessed it was partly due to her friendly flattery, and partly because of the irresistible aromas of freshly brewed coffee and cinnamon emanating from inside.

After one more moment of hesitation, the lady manoeuvred the stroller through the door. Dad looked up from his books and smiled at Annie. She winked back at him.

While Dad poured their customer a steaming cup of Earl Grey tea, Annie took the woman's coat and hung it on one of the pegs beside the bulletin board. Then she played peek-a-boo with the babies, who giggled while their mother enjoyed her drink and a cream-topped scone. Twenty minutes later, the woman was revitalized and ready to go.

Annie helped her guide her industrial-sized baby vehicle back out of the door.

"This was so nice," the young mother said, sighing. "That scone was to die for, and you have no idea how great it was to relax for a bit."

"I'm so glad you enjoyed it," Annie said sincerely. "Please come back. And tell your friends. My dad's thinking about introducing a whole menu just for little ones, actually."

Dad shot Annie a look that said, *I am?*

And Annie replied with a little nod that said, *You are now!*

"That's a wonderful idea," the mother said, reaching down to adjust the hood of the little girl's pink jumper. "Baby-friendly places are few and far between. I can't wait to tell my Mommy and Me group all about this place."

When the door closed behind their customer, Annie smiled at her dad.

"Since when do we serve baby food?" he asked, folding his arms across his chest. But he was grinning broadly and Annie could tell he was impressed by her salesmanship.

"Don't worry, Dad," she said, hurrying back to her table and tearing a sheet of paper from her notebook. "I predict those Mommy and Me ladies are going to become regulars before you can say Bob's your uncle. You saw how exhausted that woman was. She needs Rosie Lee's!"

Dad looked sceptical. "That's great, Annie, but I'm not sure a café filled with crying toddlers is going to appeal much to other customers."

"Not a problem! She won't be bringing the kids with her."

"All right … One question, though. While all those young mothers are here enjoying tea and cakes, who's going to be minding their little monsters?"

In lieu of an answer, Annie marched across the shop and pinned the sheet of notebook paper to the bulletin board with a flourish. It fluttered there for a second, stuck between an ad for a dog walker and a flyer for the community theatre's upcoming production of *Phantom of the Opera*.

"Me!" she declared.

Dad crossed the shop to read her notice.

MOVE OVER, MARY POPPINS –
THERE'S A NEW BABYSITTER IN TOWN!
VERY RESPONSIBLE, LOVES KIDS.
REASONABLE PRICES.
REFERENCES UPON REQUEST.
CALL ANNIE TURNER: 555-2702

Dad laughed out loud. "That's genius!" he cried, putting his arm around Annie and giving her a squeeze.

Then Dad and Annie went about the business of closing up for the day, wiping down the display case, rinsing out the coffee pots, sweeping the floor and closing the blinds. Annie wasn't even aware that she was whistling "A Spoonful of Sugar", the whole time.

"Need a lift to practice?" Dad asked, double-checking to be sure the coffee machine was turned off.

"Thanks, but I think I'll just skate over." Annie plopped into a chair, tugged her bulky duffle bag out from beneath the table and took out her Rollerblades. "Skating outside builds endurance, and I could do with all the help I can get."

"All right then. Lock the door behind you when you go."

Annie made quick work of lacing up her Rollerblades and putting on her pads and helmet. She also slipped into a jacket with reflective strips that glowed in the dark. With one last satisfied glance at her babysitting flyer, she turned the lock and rolled out of the door.

The feeling of the cool air on her face was exhilarating as she glided down Main Street in the direction of the roller rink. As always, she was surprised to see how many people were out and about on this quaint little street. It was hard to imagine now that when she'd first arrived in Liberty Heights she'd been worried it would be boring compared to London. But she'd met loads of interesting people.

There was a lot to learn, living in a new country, and despite her slightly rocky start, Annie believed she was finally getting the hang of it. She'd learned so many new things already, and she liked to think that some of her English ways were rubbing off on the people around her. Just yesterday, in fact, Lexie had got a B+

on a science quiz and exclaimed to Annie that the high score had her "utterly gobsmacked". Annie laughed now, remembering how funny the word had sounded in Lexie's Midwestern accent.

Strange how things turn out, she thought. As she rounded the corner that put her on the road leading to the rink, Annie felt a thrill of anticipation. She was minutes away from getting bumped, shoved, and potentially flung into a wall.

And she couldn't be happier about it!

Chapter Two

"'Sup, Anne R. Key?"

Annie smiled when she heard the friendly greeting from across the lobby. Anne R. Key was her roller derby name, chosen in homage to the Sex Pistols song "Anarchy in the UK". She glanced over and saw a familiar mop of shaggy black hair behind the rental counter. It was Jesse, manning the booth as always.

"Not much," she replied, waving. She rolled skilfully across the worn carpet and leaned her elbows on the counter. "What's up with you?"

Jesse plonked a pair of battered quad skates on the counter for Annie. She couldn't wear her Rollerblades to play roller derby.

"Just getting some music together for the next bout," he said, showing her his iPod. True to form, he'd downloaded some great old Runaways tunes, a couple of Elvis Costello classics, and an entire B-52s album. "Mainstream punk," he observed, then chuckled, his blue eyes twinkling. "That's kind of a contradiction in terms, isn't it?"

"Yes, but I know exactly what you mean." These were the names everyone thought of when they heard the term "punk rock". But Jesse, like Annie, had a far broader frame of musical reference. They were both fans of lesser known bands like Black Flag and Meat Puppets. It was one of the things she really liked about him.

Coach Ritter blew her whistle, signalling that it was time to warm up.

"Hey," said Jesse, as Annie pushed off on her skates. "You really were awesome in last week's bout against the Derby Dolls."

Annie laughed. "More like the Derby *Dulls*! But thanks. It was a great start, but we've still got a long way to go if we want to be league champs." She motioned to where the rest of the Liberty Belles were falling into line. "Which is why I'd better get moving."

As she skated away to join her teammates, she felt Jesse's eyes following her the whole way. She joined the others and took her place beside Lauren.

Lauren DeMarco was a freshman, like Annie, and also new to the world of roller derby. Lauren was Annie's "Derby Wife". Annie had found that term a bit peculiar when she'd first heard it. But she'd soon learned that it was just a funny way to describe a teammate who always had your back.

Another team, the High Rollers, were practising on the track. The noise of their collective wheels going round and round echoed through the rink, sounding like the growling of some enormous beast.

"Everybody down on the floor to stretch out," Liz, the team captain, directed.

Obediently, Annie, Lauren, and the others lowered themselves to the carpet. It was old and filthy and smelled horrid.

"I try not to think about what this rug might be contaminated with," Lauren whispered, wrinkling her nose.

"I know what you mean," Annie replied. "It's hard to know what's scarier – the High Rollers or whatever germs might be festering in this nasty old carpet."

Lauren gave an exaggerated sniff towards the grimy carpet pile. "Smells like some kind of fungus to me."

"Oh no!" Annie squealed in mock horror. "There's a fungus among us!"

"Oh, please!" Holly rolled her eyes and laughed. "A real roller girl wouldn't be put off by something as harmless as a little mould, Princess."

Holly liked to tease Annie with the nickname Princess because of her slight resemblance to Kate Middleton.

"Mould or no mould," said Liz, "never underestimate the importance of a good stretching warm up." She reached forwards over her long, muscular legs to touch the toes of her skates. "Loosen up those quadriceps, and stretch out those hip flexors. The more limber you are, the less likely you'll be to pull a muscle."

Annie knew that was true of every sport. Ten years of gymnastics had hammered that into her. Without so much as a grunt of discomfort, she arranged her legs into a wide straddle and pressed her torso outward until her chest and ribcage were flat against the floor.

A few of the other girls attempted to copy her stretch. Their efforts yielded moans of pain.

"I could try forever," Lauren sighed. "I'll never be that flexible."

"Well, it took me years to get this bendy," Annie said modestly. "And my bony bum is a bit rubbish for blocking. But that's what I like about derby. Roller girls come in all shapes and sizes."

Lauren gave Annie a grateful smile. "My mom is always telling me I'd look a lot better if I dropped a few pounds."

"I used to wish I could be petite like the girls I used to do gymnastics with," Annie replied. "I guess everyone feels self-conscious about something."

"I guess it's partly my own fault," Lauren said. "I mean, I have been going a little heavy on the Oreos and French fries lately." She shrugged. "So I don't look good in skinny jeans. But my extra pounds come in handy when I'm blocking. I know I should be more careful about eating junk food though. It's just plain unhealthy – and one of the reasons I tried out for the team was to get more healthy."

"Sounds like you've got the right attitude," Coach Ritter said with a grin. "Food is fuel. And the way we work ourselves around here, you girls need to be sure you're getting enough, and the right sort. The bottom line is, skinny jeans will eventually go out of fashion, but being healthy is always in style. If you'd like, we can bring in a nutritionist to educate us all about good dietary choices."

Lauren nodded, smiling. "That would be really helpful, Coach. Thanks."

"OK, less talking, more stretching," Liz teased.

As Annie shifted into another difficult stretch, she thought about all the delicious treats at Rosie Lee's, and how easy it was to just grab a muffin or cookie whenever her stomach started to growl. She decided she was going to have to make a bigger effort to include healthier foods in her diet. Not because she needed to lose any weight, but just because it would be better for her body in general.

Coach was blowing her whistle again – it was time to skate.

The Belles waited while the High Rollers clambered off the track for their break. Annie could see their faces glistening with sweat; they were all breathing heavily after such an intense workout, but there was a gleam in their eyes that said these girls meant business. Up close, it became clear that their team name was appropriate – the High Rollers had height on their side. One or two of them were even as tall as Annie. The High Rollers were soon assembled in a tight huddle near the wall. When the Liberty Belles had convened on the track, the Rollers broke into a loud chant, clapping in time and shouting at the top of their lungs:

"WE'RE GONNA SCREAM, WE'RE GONNA YELL,
WE'VE GOT A TEAM THAT FIGHTS LIKE HELL!
WE'RE GONNA JAM, WE'RE GONNA PASS,
NOT GONNA STOP TILL WE KICK YOUR—"

But instead of chanting the final word, the entire squad turned in unison, stuck out their backsides and gave their bums a loud smack!

"Get ready to have your butts kicked this weekend!" called the tallest girl.

"OK, Rollers, team meeting in the locker room," said their captain. Then she gave a loud war whoop and they all skated off towards the lockers in a cheering, laughing herd.

"Well, aren't *they* creative," sneered Holly, strapping her helmet on over her bright crimson hair. "That was downright poetic."

"They have a right to be cocky," Liz observed. "They did win the league last season."

"Cocky schmocky," said Sharmila, tossing her long black hair. "Someone needs to teach them some manners!" Then she waved her hand in front of her face and wrinkled her perfect nose in disgust. "And a lesson in how to apply deodorant wouldn't hurt either."

"They may smell bad," sighed Carmen, "but their derby skills don't stink."

"C'mon, let's skate," said Holly. "If we're going to beat those arrogant jerks, we've got to practise."

"*Vamonos!*" agreed Carmen. "I've got to cut out early for my shift at the store. My dad will flip if I'm late."

Practice began with the girls skating several laps, just to get their legs warm. But the High Rollers' taunts had really fired them up and the Liberty Belles' energy practically crackled in the air. Annie felt like she was part of a big, ominous thundercloud as she and her teammates circled the track. She was careful to concentrate on her form, keeping her stance low and wide for stability, with her knees deeply bent and her bum lifted as high as she could get it.

After a few laps, she could feel her lower back protesting with an ache that radiated throughout her entire core. She'd been working underused muscles and she was feeling it. Her thighs burned, too. Even though Annie was fit from gymnastics, roller derby required a completely different kind of strength. She was demanding new things of her body, but the pain was strangely satisfying.

Coach Ritter gave a blast on her whistle. "Pace line," she directed.

The girls easily arranged themselves into a tidy, single-file line. Annie giggled, thinking that derby had its own kind of supercharged choreography. Annie found herself bringing up the rear, but that was actually good news. As last in line, she would be the first to execute the drill, which consisted of weaving in and out of the swiftly moving line, like a human slalom course.

"Let's see what you've got, Turner," Coach hollered.

Annie didn't have to be told twice. She picked up speed, gaining on the girl directly in front of her, who happened to be Sharmila.

With her glossy raven hair and striking green eyes, Sharmila was one of the prettiest girls on the team, but she was every bit as tough on the track as her derby name – Sharmila the Hun – suggested.

Annie deftly cut in front of Sharmila and just as quickly darted out and forward, weaving back into line behind Carmen.

Carmen Atcha's eyes were as dark as the expensive cocoa Dad used to make his chocolate torte, and they positively sparkled with mischief.

"*Hasta la vista!*" Annie called as she flew by Carmen.

Carmen laughed. "Your accent needs work, *chica*," she hollered back. "You sound like Kate Middleton ordering enchiladas at Taco Bell!"

Annie grinned as she continued her fluid, weaving motion, in and out, down the line. She came up on Holly, who was in the zone, her head low, her eyes straight ahead. Picking up her speed a bit, Annie wove past her red-haired teammate.

Liz was at the head of the line. Annie approached, noting the definition of the muscles in her captain's arms and calves. Liz looked over her shoulder and grinned, showing Annie her chipped front tooth. She was waiting until after derby season to get it fixed. She'd told the team she thought the broken tooth made her look dangerous. But with such a friendly face, Liz was about the least scary-looking person Annie knew.

Now, Annie bent low and glided fast, rounding her captain in a smooth sweep to take the lead.

"Not bad for a freshman," Liz teased. "And a British freshman at that!"

"Hey! I'm half American!" Annie called over her shoulder.

"That must be the half that can skate!"

The pace line continued until each Belle had had her turn weaving in and out and Annie was once again last in line.

They spent the next several minutes doing hot laps for speed training. Annie was exuberant, flying around the track as though she had wings on her skates. Only Liz and Holly could keep up with her.

When Coach finally called a break, Annie's heart was pounding and she was a sticky, sweaty mess. So was everyone else.

Lauren T-stopped beside Annie, and wiped her damp brow with the back of her hand. They followed a handful of Belles to the water fountain and waited their turn. Annie had just finished drinking when she heard chanting coming from the far end of the rink. She looked up to see the High Rollers approaching from the locker room, ready for the second half of their practice.

"TWO, FOUR, SIX, EIGHT ... WHO WILL WE ASSASSINATE? BELLES! BELLES!"

"Don't they ever quit?" Lauren huffed.

The answer, apparently, was no, because the High Rollers went right on cheering: "Two, four, six, eight ... Maybe you should learn to skate! Eight, six, four, two, we can mop the floor with you!"

But surprisingly, Holly didn't rise to the bait. Instead, she turned serenely to her teammates and said, "You know, there are really only two kinds of roller girl. The ones who *are* Liberty Belles ... and the ones who want to be!"

At that the whole Liberty Belle team sent up a boisterous cheer.

Then Coach Ritter and the High Rollers' coach (whose jacket was embroidered with the name "Slammy Tammy") appeared.

They were smiling.

"You ladies certainly talk the talk," said Coach Ritter. "We were thinking maybe you'd like to walk the walk. Or maybe I should say, skate the skate."

Holly's eyes lit up. "You mean a scrimmage?"

Coach Tammy nodded. "Right here, right now."

"Bring it!" snarled the tall High Rollers girl, punching the air with a fist. When she turned to skate towards the track, Annie noticed the name on her shirt read "Dee Stroyer".

Clever.

And scary.

After some quick pre-bout strategy, the Belles took to the track. For the first jam, Annie would start as a blocker. Holly was jammer, and Liz was playing pivot.

Although there were rarely spectators at practice, Annie was suddenly aware of someone leaning over the side. She glanced up to see Jesse.

"Jesse, will you keep time?" called Coach Ritter.

He nodded and pulled a stopwatch out of his pocket, patting Annie's shoulder in an encouraging way as she skated off.

"Too bad you're gonna get creamed in front of your boyfriend," Dee Stroyer taunted, pointing in Jesse's direction and laughing as she took her position with the other blockers.

Annie decided this wasn't the time or the place to inform Dee that she and Jesse were just friends. She forced herself to focus on the task at hand, which was to block her opponents and help Holly to score. And, of course, not get killed in the bargain.

"You're going down, Belles," sneered one High Roller.

"And it ain't gonna be pretty," her teammate added.

In the next second, the rink fell still. And then…

The ref's whistle blew and the scrimmage began. The moment Annie saw her chance, she flung herself hard in the path of the High Rollers' jammer but was expertly blocked by Dee Stroyer. By some miracle, though, Holly ploughed through the pack. On Holly's next lap around, Annie and her teammates created a gap so that their jammer could sneak through, pass four High Rollers, and score four points.

As the High Rollers' jammer approached the pack, Holly slapped her hands against her hips, calling off the jam so that their opponents couldn't score any points. Then Coach Ritter pointed to Annie, and Holly passed the starred helmet panty to her. For one millisecond Annie felt a thrill of excitement as she stretched the jammer's cover over her helmet. But the thrill quickly turned to panic when she saw who was lining up beside her.

"Shouldn't you be home eating crumpets?" Dee snickered as she took her place next to Annie on the jammer line.

Annie willed herself to fire off a rude retort, but her mind was utterly blank. When the ref's whistle sounded, both girls took off like a shot, running on their toe stops.

But as Annie skated around the track, her mind raced with all the comebacks she'd been too slow to think of. Taking advantage of Annie's distraction, Dee blocked her with a particularly vicious hip check low down on her thigh, sending her out of bounds.

In the next second, Annie was sprawled on her stomach, stunned. She waited for the ref's whistle, but it didn't come. The coaches must not have noticed where Dee had hit her – anything above the shoulders or below mid thigh was illegal. Angry and embarrassed, she scrambled to her feet and stumbled back onto the track.

Annie managed to catch up with the pack, but by then, Dee Stroyer had easily taken the lead, passed through the pack a second time, scored five points, and called off the jam. Watching her high five her teammates made Annie seethe. *Shake it off,* she told herself. *Don't let that nasty girl get to you!*

Even though it was just a scrimmage, neither team showed any mercy. There was a fair amount of bruising before Coach Ritter finally signalled the end of practice.

"47-47," Slammy Tammy announced. "Good work, ladies. Based on what I saw today, I'm thinking our real bout will be a close one."

The teams went off to the locker room, exhausted, but more revved up than ever for the bout that weekend. Holly actually used the term "blood bath".

As she changed out of her sweaty gear and into her normal clothes, Annie came to a decision. *I'm not going to fall for any of those mind games again,* she vowed silently. *Come Saturday, Dee Stroyer's going to be the one who gets destroyed!*

Chapter Three

As far as Annie was concerned, Emily Brontë was proof that some of the greatest things in life came from England.

Her English teacher, Ms Schwarz, was dropping tattered paperback copies of *Wuthering Heights* onto the first desk in each row.

"Take one and pass the others back," she directed.

Annie, who was seated directly behind Tyler, waited while he accepted the three dog-eared books from the boy in front of him, kept one for himself, then turned over his shoulder to give Annie the remaining two.

When he did, Annie's breath caught in her throat. The soccer captain's eyes were so incredibly green. She wondered how Ms Brontë might describe that colour: *The dark green of moss on the*

Yorkshire Moors.

Tyler smiled as he handed over the books. "Hope this is better than *A Tale of Two Cities*," he said, referring to the last book the class had read.

Annie gulped and tried to return the smile. As she took the books, his fingers brushed hers. The contact was unintentional, she knew, but still she had to suppress the urge to let out a dreamy sigh. When he turned away, she sat staring at the back of his head for so long that the boy behind her had to tap her shoulder to remind her to pass him a book.

"Open your books to page fifty-eight," said Ms Schwarz, striding up and down the rows of desks, her batik-print skirt billowing as she went. "'He shall never know I love him: and that, not because he's handsome, but because he's more myself than I am. Whatever our souls are made out of, his and mine are the same,'" the bohemian teacher read aloud dramatically. She sighed, clutched the book to her chest, and said, "*Wuthering Heights* remains one of the greatest love stories ever told."

Wow. Emily Brontë. You go, girl! Annie gazed at the handsome soccer player sitting in front of her. Brontë's words, about Catherine's love for Heathcliff, perfectly echoed Annie's own unrequited feelings for Tyler.

"Kelsey?"

The teacher called on the captain of the cheerleader squad, whose hand was raised high in the air.

"Um, Ms Schwarz," said Kelsey in a faux-sweet tone. "I was just wondering if anyone has a tissue that Annie could use?" She nodded pointedly towards the back of Tyler's broad shoulders with a nasty grin. "She's drooling."Fortunately, only the people seated immediately around Annie made the connection. But their giggles caused Annie's cheeks to flush so ferociously she thought her face might go up in flames. She desperately wished she could disappear into the pages of Brontë's masterpiece, even if that meant she'd be stranded in the middle of a Yorkshire moor.

When Ms Schwarz told them they could spend the rest of the class reading silently, Annie lowered her head and kept her eyes firmly on her book for the rest of the lesson, even when the PA speaker erupted in a loud crackle of static.

"May I have your attention please!" the school secretary's voice burst into the room. "I have an important reminder from the social committee. Tickets for the annual Halloween dance will go on sale today. Costumes of an appropriate nature will be required in order to gain admittance to the dance."

The announcement was followed by the bell.

Kelsey was up from her seat like a shot; her cheer minions, Ginger and Lulu, in their matching miniskirts and flawless make-up, flew right to her side.

"I've got the most awesome idea for a costume!" said Ginger.

For that, Kelsey must have given her a death look, because Annie heard Ginger quickly add, "But I'm sure it won't be anywhere near as awesome as yours, Kelsey. Nobody's will be."

Seriously? Annie almost felt sorry for the girl. She may have been "popular" but she was sorely lacking in self-respect.

When Kelsey and her followers had gone, Annie finally lifted her gaze from the book.

And there were those beautiful green eyes, looking right into hers.

"So, Annie…" Tyler said, "can I ask you a question?"

She managed to gather up her things and walk to the door without fainting.

So far, so good.

When they stepped out into the crowded corridor together, Tyler had to raise his voice to be heard above the din.

"I know you haven't been here long, but you know about Halloween, right? I mean, they have that in England, don't they?"

Annie couldn't speak because another of Brontë's lines was thundering in her head: "I have to remind myself to breathe − almost to remind my heart to beat!" She answered with a nod.

"OK, cool. 'Cause there's this Halloween dance."

Annie's heart slammed into her ribs like a blocker slamming into a jammer. "Sounds lovely," she squeaked.

Tyler laughed. "Well, I don't know about lovely. But the social committee goes all out decorating the gym and everybody wears these tricked out costumes and there's a DJ."

Annie just smiled. She was already picturing herself in a long Victorian dress as Catherine, slow-dancing with Tyler, who'd be the wild and passionate Heathcliff.

Ask me, she thought. *Ask me to be your date.*

"Anyway, I was thinking it would be cool to go as David Beckham."

Tyler reached into his locker and rummaged around for a

pen. "And I was wondering if maybe you might…"

Annie held her breath … *go with you…*

"…have an authentic England football shirt I could borrow?"

So that's what this was all about? A costume? Annie felt even stupider than she had when Dee Stroyer had knocked her out of bounds in yesterday's scrimmage. Tyler didn't want to take her to the dance. He just wanted a Halloween costume.

"Sure," she heard herself say. "I think my dad has an old England strip somewhere. I'm sure he'd be OK with you borrowing it."

"Great! When will you be home so can I pick it up?"

"Hard to say. I'm kind of busy with—"

When she stopped short, he gave her a quizzical look.

It was on the tip of her tongue to say "roller derby practice". But she didn't.

"…with school work and things," she finished feebly. "But I'll try to dig it out."

"Thanks," said Tyler.

In the next second he'd been swept away in the sea of students, rushing to class, leaving Annie standing there at his locker, feeling like a complete fake.

She loved everything about roller derby, from the skating, to the excitement of competing, to the amazing friends she was making, but she hadn't wanted to admit to Tyler Erickson that she was a roller girl.

Because deep down, she suspected he wouldn't be impressed.

Worse, he might even think she was some kind of freaky

fishnet-wearing loser.

And the fact that she cared about that even a little was the worst feeling of all.

Lexie was already banging open her locker when Annie arrived. She immediately noticed Annie's glum expression.

"Let me guess," Lexie teased, "you got a D on your algebra homework?"

"I'm fine," Annie lied. "But I was wondering … are you going to this Halloween dance?"

Lexi let out a little snort of laughter. "*Moi?* At a school dance? Have you met me?" To make her point, she gave a little twirl, showing off her African-print dress in a nod to her half-African ancestry. Her curly hair was hidden beneath an intricately wrapped scarf and her gold hoop earrings were large enough for circus poodles to jump through. "I'm not exactly a candidate for prom queen."

Annie had been afraid of that. Lexie was artsy and a bit of a rebel. Annie should have known mainstream clichés like school dances wouldn't appeal to her. But still…

"I know they're naff," Annie said. "But just this once, it might be fun. They seem like a big deal in all the American teen movies I've seen."

"Clearly you haven't seen *Carrie*. Now *there's* a school dance you'd probably want to skip!" Lexie gave her an understanding smile, hoisting the strap of her enormous art portfolio onto her shoulder. "Look, I get it. But trust me, real school dances generally don't measure up to the ones on the big screen. We had dances in middle school all the time. Naturally, I was a conscientious objector, but my mom insisted I go to a few. The girls were lined up on one side of the gym, pretending their training bras weren't stuffed with tissues, and the boys lined up on the other, hoping their voices wouldn't crack when they asked a girl to dance. I actually saw one kid pop a zit right into the punch bowl."

"Yuuccckkk."

Lexie nodded. "Now you're getting it. And consider this: the music. Pop tunes, *more* pop tunes, and nothing *but* pop tunes."

Annie sighed. "But that was middle school. Won't a high school dance be better?"

"Maybe," Lexie said. "I mean, for one thing, the boobs'll be real. Well, most of them, anyway. And I don't completely hate the idea of everyone going in costume. I mean, maybe for once, I wouldn't be the one sporting the most outrageous look in the room."

"See? There's that." Annie opened her own locker and pulled out her algebra book. "Promise me you'll consider going?" she said in a hopeful tone.

"I promise."

They made plans to meet for lunch in the cafeteria and Lexie headed down the hall towards the art room with Aaron, a friend from her class with dyed black hair and a nose ring.

As Annie closed her locker, she sent up a silent prayer that her best friend would agree to go to the dance with her.

Because one thing was for certain: Tyler wasn't about to ask her.

Chapter Four

Annie entered the rink on Saturday evening to the sound of The Clash rocking the place. That meant Jesse was operating the sound system, and this made her smile. Jesse shared her taste in music and it was nice to have someone to talk "punk" with.

She found him fiddling with the speakers. "Hey, you."

He looked up from the wiring and grinned. "Well, if it isn't our very own British Invasion."

Annie laughed. "Oh, so that's how you think of me, then? As an invader?"

For a second, Jesse's expression was unreadable, then he laughed, too. "Nah. We're lucky to have you on American soil, the Liberty Belles especially."

"Hmm." Annie rolled her eyes. "After my face plant during

Thursday's scrimmage, I'm not so sure."

"It happens," Jesse assured her. "You're a great player. Don't let that stuff get you down. It's all just part of the game."

A cheerful voice boomed across the rink. "Annie, c'mere!"

Annie turned to see Sharmila waving her towards the lockers, holding a pot of glitter gel.

"Time to get your war paint on," said Jesse.

Annie shook her head thoughtfully. "Funny, I've worn more make-up since I became a roller girl than I've worn in my whole life put together."

"Well, you don't need make-up," Jesse said matter-of-factly. "You're more than pretty enough without it."

The compliment seemed to surprise him as much as it did Annie. His cheeks turned pink and he quickly shifted his gaze back to the speakers, clearing his throat. "But, ya know, everyone can benefit from a little glitter now and then."

Annie bit back a smile. She'd taken only three steps towards the lockers when Jesse said, "Annie?"

She stopped and turned around to face him again. "Yes?"

"I, uh, I downloaded a special playlist, with you in mind. I'm gonna play it during warm-ups, to help get you psyched."

"I'll definitely listen out for it. Thanks, Jesse."

"No, problem."

Annie hurried towards the lockers to get ready.

* * *

"Do these blue fishnets clash with my pink shorts?" asked Holly.

"Anybody have an extra pair of false eyelashes I can borrow?" called Liz.

"Take mine. I'm just going with some purple mascara tonight!" replied Carmen.

Annie watched as Lauren ducked to avoid the tube of eyelash adhesive that sailed over her head; Carmen had thrown it to Liz, who caught it easily.

"Thanks, Carm."

"No prob. Just don't get that glue in your eyes. It stings like crazy!"

Annie couldn't help giggling as she allowed Sharmila to powder her eyelids with the sparkling eyeshadow. Back when she was an elite gymnast, Annie had spent plenty of time getting ready in the locker room. Gymnasts did wear a fair amount of blush and lip gloss and even glitter hairspray for meets. But roller derby make-up was an entirely different art form – more like warpaint. Part glam, part monster movie, it featured heavily lined eyes and scary embellishments.

"This looks incredible on you," Sharmila announced, sitting back to admire her handiwork. "It really brings out your eyes."

"Thanks," said Annie, blinking at her reflection. She actually did look glamorous – in a truly terrifying sort of way! In addition to the orange glitter shadow, Sharmila had heavily outlined her eyes with swampy green liner and applied a thick coat of mascara. Then she'd added a series of black thunderbolts along her jawline and a long, purple "scar" across her forehead. She also wrote Annie's player number – 5'11"½ – on her arm in bold black numbers with a marker pen. Annie had chosen it as a reference to her height, which in roller derby (unlike in gymnastics), was turning out to be an advantage.

Sharmila had gone a little off the rails with her own make-up. Rather than playing up her stunning features with eyeliner and lipstick, she'd created a virtual mask with black and white face paint. She looked like a weird hybrid of skeleton and supermodel.

"Are you sure you don't want to go a little sexier with your outfit?" Sharmila asked, eyeing Annie's black tights and snug red miniskirt.

"Sexier than a skirt made of less fabric than a handkerchief?" Annie looked down at her long legs emerging from the tiny Lycra skirt and laughed. "I'm good, thanks."

"Why settle for good when you could look great?" Holly snapped. She adjusted her torn T-shirt to better reveal the impressive cleavage created by her turquoise bra. "If you've got it, flaunt it, Princess." To illustrate her point, she did a sultry hip circle, showing off her shiny satin shorts.

Annie had to admit, Holly would attract a lot of attention in that outfit. Maybe as the season progressed, Annie would vamp up her own look a bit, but for now she was content with the skirt and team T-shirt with her derby name printed across the back.

Annie made her way across the locker room to where Lauren was using a sticky hair gel to spike up her short, brown hair.

"What do you think?" Lauren asked, gingerly patting

at the points with her palm. "Do I look like a burnt lemon meringue pie?"

"More like a porcupine with highlights," Annie giggled.

"I can live with that," Lauren said, grinning. Then she struck an exaggerated body-builder pose, flexing her biceps. "So what do you think of *these*?"

Annie's eyes widened when she realized what Lauren was showing her: a dragon tattoo on her left arm, and a skull and crossbones tattoo on her right. "Lauren, you didn't!"

Lauren laughed. "Of course I didn't. My mom would never let me get inked. These are just the temporary kind."

Annie let out a sigh of relief, leaning in for a closer look. "They look so real."

Then Coach Ritter appeared in the doorway to tell them it was time.

Annie could hear Jesse's musical tribute to her blaring through the locker room door. It was The Clash's "London's Burning".

"Let's hear it, Belles!" Liz commanded, pumping her fist in the air.

The girls exploded into whoops and hollers. As they rolled out of the locker room, they deepened their voices to a more menacing octave and chanted, "Belles, Belles, Belles!"

Annie's heart was racing; she remembered the crowds of fans who had cheered so exuberantly for the Illinoisies when she and Lexie had gone to see the local adult roller derby team play. She couldn't wait to feel the rink vibrate with the same thunderous applause.

As she and her teammates skated around the track, Annie scanned the crowd. Dad had been recruited by Coach Ritter to be the penalty box timekeeper.

The rest of the fans clapped and cheered.

All *six* of them.

A middle-aged couple (probably someone's parents), a couple of boys wearing baseball jackets from a private high school across town, a boy in a leather jacket with black hair ... and one girl in a skull and crossbones-patterned headscarf wearing huge hoop earrings. Lexie!

Annie's heart swelled with gratitude for her friend's loyalty. On closer inspection, the boy in the leather jacket was Lexie's friend Aaron. But happy as she was to see them, Annie wished there were more people there to cheer them on. She thought of the masses of die-hard fans who attended football matches back in the UK, sporting team colours and painted faces. Sometimes those fans got a bit rowdy, but all things considered, Annie would have much preferred a little spirited mischief to the empty rink.

Maybe it doesn't fill up until just before the bout starts, she thought. She glanced into the stands, where Lexie was cheering louder than the other five spectators put together.

Maybe there's traffic?

A long queue at the snack bar?

But from the looks on the other girls' faces, Annie realized that they were disappointed by tonight's turnout too.

Annie's heart sank.

"I don't get it," she said, executing a toe stop and frowning.

"There were plenty of people at our last bout."

Holly rolled her eyes. "Do you think *maybe* it could have anything to do with the fact that there's a Liberty Heights High soccer game tonight?"

Annie sighed. "I forgot about that."

"Everybody goes to the home soccer games," Liz explained, joining them. "I guess you can't blame them. The team is really good. And there's a bonfire, and, of course, cheerleaders."

Ugh. Annie felt a little queasy at the mention of that. Especially as it meant that Kelsey was there, cheering Tyler on.

"Please!" huffed Holly. "We are so much hotter than those Barbie dolls with pom-poms for brains. You'd think people would be breaking down the doors to watch us skate!"

"They might," said Carmen, shooting her a grin, "if they knew how much cleavage you were showing."

"Look," said Liz, "we can worry about drumming up spectators later. But right now, we've got a bout to win!"

Liz was right. The girls skated to the side of the track to await their introductions. Then Jesse's voice came crackling over the loudspeaker: "Who's ready for some derby action?"

Well, at least Lexie was! She leaped to her feet and whooped like a mad woman. The other four patrons clapped and hollered, but remained seated.

"Here they are, ladies and gentlemen... Your very own Liberty Belles! Put your hands together for team captain, ElizaDEATH, who's come back from beyond the grave to entertain us tonight!"

Liz barrelled onto the track, waving to the "legions" of fans

47

in the stands.

Glory hog that she was, Holly didn't wait to be announced. Before Jesse could introduce her, she burst out behind Liz and began showing off her moves.

But Jesse didn't miss a beat. "Crashing the party as always, here comes our resident bad girl, the one and only Holly Terror!"

Holly's antics managed to fire up the tiny crowd a bit, and Annie took satisfaction in the fact that the Derby Dolls looked intimidated by her teammate's skills.

"And now," Jesse was saying, "here's the senorita-who-will-beat-ya! Look out, folks, 'cause she's Carmen Atcha!"

Annie laughed as Carmen skated on, impressed with Jesse's clever wit. She wondered what he'd say when her turn came.

"And who needs the police when we've got our very own Lauren Disorder?"

When Lauren took to the track, the middle-aged couple went wild. *Obviously her parents*, Annie thought.

Sharmila was next. Jesse made his voice frantic. "The barbarians are attacking! Prepare to be stunned by the stunning Sharmila the Hun!"

Annie was surprised at the weird tug of jealousy she felt hearing Jesse refer to Sharmila as stunning. It was true of course – Sharmila was a knock out. So why did Annie feel bothered by it?

But then Jesse was drawling into the mic, "Somebody call Paul Revere! The British are coming! We don't want no monarchy! We want total *Anne R. Key!*"

Exhilarated, Annie zoomed onto the track, skating at full speed as the music segued into what Jesse had clearly decided was her personal theme song, "Anarchy in the UK". Annie revelled in the rush of air in her face as she pushed herself to go faster; it seemed to be whistling along with the lyrics: "Don't know what I want but I know how to get it…"

Lexie was on her feet again, screaming like crazy.

After Jesse had introduced the rest of the Belles, he moved on to the Derby Dolls. Technically, as the announcer, he was supposed to be impartial, but as he rattled off the names of the other team Annie notice that his puns weren't as inspired and his delivery was less enthusiastic.

Good. She preferred it that way.

And then the whistle blew and it was time for action.

The lack of fans didn't seem to hinder the players' energy levels. The first jam was fast and furious. Liz was pivot and she barked out the strategies, skilfully anticipating their opponents' next moves. Annie was awed by the way her captain always seemed to be one step ahead of them; she was truly an instinctive player.

For Annie's part, what she lacked in experience she more than made up for in speed. She easily kept up with the wall, zipping around the track and watching with envy as Holly, jammer extraordinaire, bombed through the pack, dodging the opposing blockers to score again and again.

Lauren, too, was in good form, showing just how powerful she was.

When Annie took her place in the pack for the second jam, she realized that the Derby Dolls' jammer was in her English class. According to the girl's T-shirt, her name was Tessa Distress-a.

Annie had only one goal in mind – to block Tessa right into oblivion! With her head down and her bum in the air, Annie resolved to keep Tessa from getting past. But that meant Annie forgot to check where the rest of the pack was.

"Annie – twenty-foot rule!" Liz's voice rose in warning above the gravelly whirr of the skates on the floor. "Twenty-foot rule!"

Annie looked up and saw that she'd fallen so far behind the other skaters in the pack that she was in danger of violating the rule that said blockers couldn't be more than twenty feet away from the front or back of the pack. She scrambled to catch up with them but the ref's whistle screeched.

Pointing an accusing finger at Annie, he barked, "Penalty!"

Annie made her way to the sin bin, where Dad was acting as timekeeper, to serve her one minute timeout.

After starting the timer on his stopwatch, Dad gave her a little pep talk. "Think of this as a chance to catch your breath and plan your strategy," he advised. "When I pop a batch of cupcakes in the oven, I use the time they're baking to brainstorm and come up with new recipes."

"So you're comparing me to a cupcake right now?"

Dad grinned. "Yes, I suppose I am!"

Dad's advice was sound. As Annie sat in the penalty box, she devoured the action on the track with her eyes and mind, studying Holly's and Liz's expert moves and strategies. Some of the Derby Dolls were worth watching, too.

Her brain ticked as she watched Carmen grab onto Sharmila's waist, then catapult herself forward.

She watched Holly dodge and weave, as aggressive as a wolf on the hunt, but as graceful as a figure skater.

Finally, Dad's stopwatch beeped. Annie's penalty ended and she bolted back out to join the pack.

"Waterfall!" Lauren commanded, reaching out to grab Annie's hands. Annie caught Lauren's and held tight, easily blocking the Dolls' jammer.

And then it was finally Annie's turn to be jammer. Her adrenaline rush combined with the mental notes she'd taken while serving time in the penalty box proved to be a dazzling combination. She racked up point after point after *point*!

"Anne R. Key scores again!" Jesse announced. The next time she scored, he played the Ramones' "Blitzkrieg Bop" in celebration of her success.

The Liberty Belles continued to play well for the whole bout. When the final whistle blew, they'd won by 111-69 points.

And Annie Turner, aka Anne R. Key, took great pleasure in knowing she'd had a lot to do with it!

Chapter Five

The mood in the locker room was bittersweet. The Belles were thrilled to have won so resoundingly, but the fact that there'd been barely anyone there to witness their victory was a major downer.

"So let's put our heads together," Liz suggested, "and come up with a way to get some butts in those seats."

"Derby is about showmanship," Annie said, thinking out loud. "Maybe we can capitalize on that."

"What do you mean?" said Holly, sarcasm dripping from her tone. "In between jams we can tap dance, juggle ... maybe even hold a sing-a-long?"

"We could do giveaways," Lauren suggested. "You know, like the first hundred people in the door get a prize."

"Like a date with Sharmila?" Carmen said, giggling. "The boys would totally line up for that."

"I was thinking more along the lines of a travel mug with our logo on it."

"Oh, right," scoffed Holly, "because we have a whole storeroom filled with mugs." She tugged off her torn T-shirt and flung it into her duffle bag. "Those things cost money, which in case you didn't notice, we don't have."

"Don't listen to her, Lauren," Annie said firmly. "It was a good idea."

"I agree," said Coach Ritter, appearing from behind a bank of lockers to frown at Holly. "Teamwork doesn't just count on the track, Holly. So how about a little less negativity, and a little more respect for your teammates."

Holly nodded, chastised.

"Annie, what exactly did you mean by showmanship?" Liz asked. She was removing the elastic band that held her hair in its tight French plait. "That sounded promising."

"I guess I was thinking we might add some kind of theatrical element," Annie explained.

"But what?" asked Sharmila. She was using make-up remover to wipe the chalky black and white paint from her face. With half of her skeleton face paint smeared off, Sharmila looked downright terrifying – like a zombie whose face was melting.

Inspiration struck. "Halloween!" cried Annie.

Carmen shrugged. "Yeah, what about it?"

"We can have a special, Halloween-themed bout! Instead of

our usual uniforms, we can wear spooky costumes and go all out with the monster make-up. The audience can come in costumes, too, and we can even give out sweets between jams. I bet Jesse could find some really cool Halloween music!"

Coach Ritter smiled. "I think that's a wonderful idea."

"So do I," said Liz. "I'll talk to Allison Daniels. She's captain of the High Rollers."

"Well, if she's anything like her teammate Dee Stroyer," Lauren cautioned, "you might want to bring along backup."

"Nah." Liz smiled. "Allie's nice. And she's a good sport – I'm sure she'll be up for an expedition bout."

"I'll do everyone's make-up," Sharmila volunteered, her gorgeous face now devoid of greasepaint. "Not sure I can make this one any scarier than she already is," she teased, taking Holly's chin in her hand, "but I'll give it my best shot."

Holly just laughed and stuck out her tongue.

"What about costumes?" asked Lauren. "I was planning to be a cat for Halloween, but something tells me that won't cut it."

"I think we should all be the same thing, only different," said Annie. "Like, say we all dress as vampires. But we can all have an individual persona. Someone can be a nerdy vampire, someone else can be a baby vampire…"

"I'll be a sexy vampire," said Holly.

Liz laughed. "There's a surprise."

"What about the High Rollers?" Liz asked. "I'll have to tell Allie how they should dress. What do you think they should be?"

"How about witches?" Annie suggested. "After all, that Dee

Stroyer's already halfway there."

Everyone cracked up at that. As the girls brainstormed ideas for songs, posters, and costumes, any gloom they'd been feeling vanished entirely.

And now Annie was more excited than ever for her first American Halloween.

Lexie's pencil flew across the paper as though she were possessed. Annie sipped her hot chocolate and watched in awe as images appeared on the blank page beneath Lexie's hands. As she had with the mural in Rosie Lee's, Lexie was creating something out of nothing.

And the something was an array of vampire personas.

They were sitting in the kitchen of Annie's house, which had belonged to her grandparents and, sadly, had not enjoyed a decorating update in decades. Lexie, of course, loved the dated 1980s wallpaper and lino. She called it "retro". Annie just called it naff.

"You're sure you don't mind designing our costumes for the bout?" Annie asked. Lexie had agreed to do it the moment Annie had asked – in fact she'd accepted before Annie had fully finished speaking. This was the sort of project Lexie lived for. But Annie wanted to be certain she wasn't taking advantage of her best friend's time or talents.

"I told you," Lexie said, flipping her pencil over to erase an errant line. "I want to do it. I'm not usually a joiner, as you know, but this is something I can totally rock." She blew the rubbings off the page, made her correction, and held up her sketch. "Sexy Vampiress," she announced.

"Lexie!" Annie's eyes went round with admiration. "That's brilliant!"

"Not showing too much skin, is it?"

Annie laughed. "You've been to bouts before. You know roller girls aren't exactly a modest lot."

"Good," said Lexie, putting down the pad and reaching for her own hot chocolate. "Because this is gonna look ah-mazing on you!"

"Me?" Annie nearly choked on her mouthful of drink. "No. No way. I was thinking I'd be the sporty vampire, or maybe the nerdy one. Definitely not the sexy one. Besides, Holly already called dibs on it."

"Dibs?" Lexie rolled her eyes. "What are we, in third grade? What's she gonna do if *you* decide to be the sexy one? Refuse to go on the seesaw with you at recess?"

Annie laughed. "OK, OK, I get it."

"Besides, Holly may have that whole 'naughty girl' thing going on but trust me, she'll never be able to pull off what I have in mind." Lexie indicated the bottom half of the drawing. "See? This costume is designed for long legs like yours. Check out the slit up the side."

Annie squinted at the drawing. "Oh, wow. That is revealing."

"What's revealing?" asked Dad, popping in from the

family room.

Blushing, Annie snatched the drawing from Lexie and covered the sexy vampire sketch with a napkin.

"Uh, nothing."

"I'm glad you girls are here," said Dad, going to the fridge to remove a jug of sweet apple cider. "I could use a little help." As he poured himself a glass, the tart, sweet smell of apples filled the kitchen. "Business, as you know, is not exactly booming. I need to get people into Rosie Lee's and I need to get 'em there soon."

"Sounds like Rosie Lee's and the Liberty Belles are having the same problem," Lexie observed.

Annie raised her eyebrows. If Lexie even so much as *hinted* that Annie's dad should show up at the café dressed as a sexy vampire, she'd kill her!

"Exactly," said Dad. "And like the Belles, I'm going to try and solve that problem by tapping into the Halloween spirit." He joined them at the table, sipping his drink. Dad's eyes twinkled as he shot a look at Annie. "Tell me, does the high school still throw its annual Halloween dance?"

Annie lifted one shoulder in a half shrug. "I may have heard something about such an event," she hedged.

Dad chuckled. "Well, have you two lovely ladies decided which lucky lads are going to have the privilege of escorting you?"

"Uhhh – *no*." Lexie wrinkled her nose. "See, I usually make it a point to avoid any teenage social ritual that includes crêpe paper streamers and punch."

"How about you, String Bean? Do you want to go?"

Yes, I want to go more than anything! I want to go with Tyler Erikson, the most beautiful boy on the planet.

"Hadn't really given it much thought."

"Really?" Dad seemed surprised.

"Well…" Annie nonchalantly swirled the chocolatey liquid in her mug. "I mean, maybe if somebody asks me, I'll think about it."

"Hmm." Dad looked as though he might want to say more on the topic, but instead, he turned to back to Lexie.

"I seem to recall that the trick-or-treating here in Liberty Heights is second to none. Is that still the case?"

"Absolutely," said Lexie. "People are totally into it. They give out candy by the bucketful. And not those wimpy little fun-size bars, either. The big ones! People practically wage war over who's got the best decorations. They throw open-house parties, and hold pumpkin-carving contests."

"I was counting on that," said Dad. "Which is why I'm going to create a whole spook-inspired Halloween menu."

"Hey, that's a fabulous idea!" cried Annie. "People will come in to buy treats for their parties, and they'll probably stay for a scone and a cup of hot chocolate."

"Or hot mulled cider," Dad said, smacking his lips as he finished his drink. "I was hoping you two geniuses would have a few ideas for me."

"Spooky food, huh?" Lexie frowned in thought. "Well, personally, I don't think there's anything scarier than my mom's tofu veggie lasagne, but I don't think that's the kind of scary you had in mind."

"I have an idea," said Annie. "What if you baked brownies with maraschino cherries in the mix?"

"That's not scary," said Dad.

"It is if you call them blood clot brownies!"

"Uck. I believe you're right." Dad picked up Lexie's abandoned pencil, then reached for the napkin that concealed the vampire-meets-glamour-model sketch. Annie gasped, but luckily, Dad seemed too intent on scribbling "blood clot brownies" on the napkin to notice the risqué drawing. "What else have you got?"

"Lady fingers," Lexie proposed. "Ones that look like an actual lady's fingers, chopped off an actual lady's hands. You can use red icing to make them really gory."

"Excellent."

"How about mummified gingerbread boys?" said Annie.

"I like it!"

Half an hour later, Dad had a list of horrifyingly delicious treats to add to his repertoire. He wasn't too sure about Lexie's idea for cupcakes with vomit filling (apple sauce with chunky chocolate chips and coconut flakes stirred in) but he promised to think about it.

"Thanks for all your help," he said, tucking the napkin with his notes into his shirt pocket. Then leaned back in his chair with a wistful expression on his face. "Annie, do you remember the first time Mum and I took you trick-or-treating in London?"

Annie nodded. "I went as a lobster, right?"

Dad nodded. "Mum was a real trooper. She knew the neighbours would think we were nuts. Still, she went along with it anyway, patiently explaining to all our confused neighbours why we were standing on their doorsteps asking for candy, with our three-year-old daughter dressed up as a crustacean." He laughed, but his eyes were sad. "No one had any candy to put in your bag, but I remember Mr Harrison gave you a handful of cough drops. And old Mrs Bentley gave you some shortbread she'd just baked."

Annie closed her eyes. She could almost smell that shortbread, sweet and hot from the oven. Not for the first time, she wondered if Dad missing Mum was a first step towards them working things out. Of course, the fact that Mum hadn't even called for a week didn't bode well for that possibility.

There was a lump in her throat as she brought her mug to her lips.

"You sure made an awfully cute lobster," Dad said softly. Then he sighed and stood up abruptly. "I guess I'd better start looking up recipes for these devilish desserts."

"Good luck," Lexie called after him.

He was halfway to the door when he turned to look over his shoulder at Annie.

"Oh … and about that vampire outfit…" he said casually. "If you shave a good three inches off the length of that slit, and maybe bring up the neckline a bit, I might actually consider letting you wear it."

For the second time that evening Annie almost gagged on her hot chocolate.

"Oh … um … right … okay," she managed to choke out. "We'll see what we can do."

"Good," said Dad. "Or else you'll be going as a lobster again."

At that, Lexie burst out laughing.

But Annie had a sneaking suspicion that he wasn't kidding.

Chapter Six

The next morning, while Annie stood at her locker searching for her biology textbook, she was amazed at the swirl of dance-related gossip that filled the corridor.

Not surprisingly, it seemed that most of the cheerleaders had been asked to the dance by soccer and football players. The drama club kids appeared to be more excited about what costumes they'd be wearing than who they'd actually be going with. An uber-shy sophomore boy had asked a very popular senior girl and to everyone's shock she'd agreed to go with him!

Annie finally found her book and set out down the hall towards class. She had to dodge a few ladders along the way, since the social committee was hard at work hanging up posters for the dance. One huge banner caught her eye. It was painted in black and orange and had a picture of Freddy Kruger on it.

GET YOUR SCARE ON AT THE HALLOWEEN DANCE. MISSING IT WOULD BE A NIGHTMARE!

The time and date were written beneath the picture in dripping, blood-red letters. This triggered something in Annie's mind, but she was too preoccupied with the dance gossip buzzing around to make any real connection.

When Annie reached the science classroom, she slid into her seat and tried to imagine what it would be like to go to the dance with Tyler. He was going as David Beckham. Maybe she could go as Victoria Beckham! All she would need would be a little black bobbed wig, a really sexy dress, and super-high heels.

"Open your texts to page twenty-seven," Mr Dinkins, the biology teacher, instructed. "Today we will be diagramming plant cells."

Dutifully, Annie began sketching. She drew the blob-shaped outline, careful to differentiate the cell wall from the cell membrane. But try as she might, she just couldn't focus on mitochondrion and Golgi vesicles. Her mind – and her pencil – began to wander and before she knew it, she'd doodled "Tyler Erickson" in block print, bubble letters, and loopy script all over her margins.

She even drew a heart with their initials inside!

When she realized what she'd done, she quickly erased it. *I need to stop being so soppy over a boy who barely knows I'm alive,* she chastised herself, brushing the eraser crumbs off her notebook.

She spent the rest of the lesson determinedly memorizing the function of the vacuole membrane and pushing Tyler's green eyes and heart-melting smile out of her mind.

The rest of her morning classes passed in a similar fashion.

In History, she struggled to pay attention, but every time the teacher told them to remember a particular date for the upcoming quiz, her mind flew directly to the other kind of date.

In French, she gave up working on verb tenses and instead conjugated the verb "*danser*": to dance.

In Algebra, they had a substitute teacher who gave them an easy worksheet and told them they could talk quietly amongst themselves when they'd completed it.

When Annie returned to her seat after dropping her finished worksheet on the teacher's desk, the girl who sat behind her leaned forward. Her name was Emily and she was on the girls' soccer team.

"So what are you going to be for Halloween?" Emily whispered.

"Not sure yet," said Annie. On the chance that Emily might attend the Liberty Belle's themed bout, she didn't want to spill the beans about the entire team dressing up as vampires. "How about you?"

"Well…" Emily sighed. "I'm torn between going as a cowgirl – you know, with boots and a hat and all – and a mermaid."

"It'll be too hard to dance in a mermaid tail," said the girl next to Emily. Her name was Jessica and she had also tried out for cheerleading. She hadn't made it on the first go, but Annie's "resignation" had bumped her up to a place on the squad. For this reason, Jessica (unlike the other cheerleaders) seemed to feel beholden to Annie and treated her nicely.

"She has a point," Annie agreed, giggling. "What's your costume, Jessica?"

"My boyfriend and I are going as Frankenstein and his bride," Jessica grumbled. "His idea, not mine. I was hoping for something cuter, like maybe Cinderella and Prince Charming, but... Oh!" suddenly Jessica's eyes lit up. "Speaking of Prince Charming ... Annie, you know who you should go as, don't you?"

Annie shook her head.

"Kate what's-her-name. You know, the one who married Prince William!"

"Kate Middleton?" Annie asked.

Emily nodded enthusiastically. "It's perfect! I mean you look kind of similar! Same hair, and you're tall and slim like her."

And Tyler would make the perfect Prince William, she thought, blushing. Quickly, she shook her head. She really needed to stop daydreaming about that.

When the class bell rang, Annie headed directly for the cafeteria to meet Lexie and Lauren. She made it through the hot lunch queue in record time, and put her tray down across from Lexie, who was biting into a tuna sandwich.

"Pizza," she observed, nodding at Annie's lunch selection.

"Brave choice."

Annie frowned. "Why's that?"

"Well, for one thing, there's enough grease in one of those pepperoni slices to keep the acne cream manufacturers in business until the next millennium. And that cheese..." She shook her head slowly. "Probably not actually cheese."

"Don't listen to her," sighed Lauren. "She's kidding."

Annie glanced at Lexie, who laughed. "Yeah, I'm just joking. The pizza is actually one of their better offerings. However, do yourself a favour and avoid the fried fish filet sandwich at all costs."

Lauren grinned. "The tartar sauce alone could kill you."

"Well, if you're sure it's safe..." Annie gave them a teasing look, then opened her mouth as wide as she could and took an enormous bite of her pizza. She was only being silly – usually her table manners were better than this. The pepperoni was yummy, the sauce tangy, and the cheese – real or not – was gooey and delicious.

Suddenly, Lexie's eyes went wide. "OMG," she whispered. "Tyler is walking over!"

Annie kept chewing her huge mouthful and rolled her eyes.

"No!" cried Lexie. "I'm serious."

"She's telling the truth," Lauren confirmed, quickly reaching out with a napkin to wipe a glob of tomato sauce from Annie's chin. "He's walking right toward us. I mean ... *you!*"

Annie's stomach flipped. Why would Tyler be heading towards her? And why had she chosen this moment to experiment with visual comedy by taking a glutton-sized chomp of her pizza?

She stopped chewing and looked up to see Tyler standing beside her.

"Hi, Annie," he said.

If she opened her mouth, an avalanche of half-chewed pizza would have spilled out. So she gave him a closed-lip smile and nodded. Lexie and Lauren looked torn between feeling sorry for her and ready to burst out laughing.

"Listen," he began with that winning smile. "I should have asked you this the other day when we were talking about costumes and all. I really hope someone hasn't beaten me to it."

Since Annie still couldn't speak without sputtering globs of cheese and pepperoni all over the place, she raised her eyebrows and inclined her head in a curious gesture.

"Would you like to go to the Halloween dance with me?"

It was all Annie could do to keep from jumping out of her chair and throwing her arms around him. Between the giant mouthful of pizza-flavoured mush and the shock of being asked out by Tyler, she was lucky she didn't choke to death!

The answer, of course, was a resounding yes. She only wished she could say it!

What to do?

Nod? No, way too impersonal.

She considered picking up a napkin and spitting the offending mouthful into it, but what could possibly be more disgusting than that?

Annie could feel her face turning pink as Tyler looked down

at her expectantly.

Luckily, she was spared because at that moment, one of Tyler's buddies appeared at his side.

"Dude, let's jet," he said, throwing a friendly punch to Tyler's shoulder. "We've got class on the other side of the building. One more tardy and we both get detention and miss the game."

Tyler gave Annie an adorable shrug. "Gotta motor. Let's catch up later and we can talk about it then."

When he was gone, Lauren hastily handed Annie a napkin and Annie spit the horrible wad of half-chewed pizza into it.

"Well, that was romantic wasn't it?" Lexie teased.

Annie groaned and dropped her head onto the table. "Tell me that really didn't happen."

"Oh, it happened," said Lauren. "And judging from the way Kelsey is staring daggers at you from the cool lunch table, there are witnesses who can testify to it."

Annie lifted her head and sneaked a glance at Kelsey. Lauren was right. Kelsey had seen Tyler talking to Annie, and she obviously had a good idea of what he was asking her. She looked furious.

"Call me crazy, but I would call that an upside," said Lexie.

Annie had to admit, she did feel a tiny thrill of victory at being chosen by Tyler over the head cheerleader. But truthfully, that was the least of it. She genuinely liked him. And he liked her! At least enough to want to take her to the dance.

A dazed and happy look must have come over Annie's face because Lauren giggled and Lexie rolled her eyes.

"I don't know if you can hear me over the violins playing in your head," Lexie teased, reaching across the table towards Annie's plate. "But something tells me I might as well finish your pizza."

Pizza? What pizza? She was going to the Halloween dance with Tyler!

Dodge ball. Without a doubt the stupidest American sport ever invented.

In fact, in Annie's opinion, it shouldn't even qualify as a sport. As far as she was concerned it was mean-spirited and aggressive, with no redeeming athletic qualities whatsoever.

She mentioned this to Lexie for the fifteenth time, as they stood with the rest of their team on one side of the gymnasium.

"I find it hard to believe that the same school that sent home a six-page letter about its zero tolerance policy on bullying actually allows this behaviour." Annie tossed the red rubber ball half-heartedly into the cluster of opponents whose job it was to dodge it. "Kids intentionally hurling things at other kids? What do they call that?"

"They call it Phys. Ed.," said Lexie, ducking to avoid the ball. "All in the name of personal well-being and good health."

The minute the words left her mouth, a skinny boy named Travis took a ball to the face, resulting in a minor nose bleed.

Annie felt sorry for him, but truth be told, it would be difficult for anything – dodge ball and bloody noses included – to interfere with her good mood right now.

She was still flying high over the idea that she would be attending the Halloween dance on the arm of Tyler Erickson. All that was left was to officially accept his invitation, which she planned to do the next time she saw him. *Here come Posh and Becks,* she thought, imagining their costumes.

The gym teacher blew her whistle and the teams switched places.

"Keep your head in the game," Lexie advised. "I know you're all dreamy over Mr Wonderful, but you don't want to wind up with a black eye or a fat lip."

True. That would definitely clash with her glamorous Victoria Beckham look.

She managed to keep from getting hit by a ball for the first five minutes of play, but she got distracted when she spotted some social committee members climbing the tiered seats to hang up yet another poster advertising the dance.

This sign didn't have a creepy horror movie character on it; it was simple and to the point.

DON'T MISS THE HALLOWEEN DANCE
LIBERTY HEIGHTS HIGH SCHOOL GYMNASIUM
SATURDAY, OCTOBER 31 8.00 P.M.

Annie froze where she stood on the gym floor.

Saturday?

October 31st!

That's what had been niggling at her when she'd seen the first banner that morning.

"Oh no," she said. "No, please tell me that's a misprint!"

"What's the matter?" asked Lexie, ducking to avoid being clobbered by a ball.

"I thought the dance was going to be on Friday night!"

Lexie followed Annie's horrified gaze to the sign on the wall. "Saturday's the night of your Halloween bout, isn't it?"

Annie nodded.

"I didn't realize," said Lexie, sidestepping another ball. "I guess I didn't pay any attention to the signs since I was never planning to go."

Annie couldn't bring herself to move; she just stood there staring at the sign.

Which was why she didn't see the ball zooming towards her.

It hit her in the stomach so hard, she actually doubled over.

"You're out!" called the gym teacher, with a blast on his whistle.

That was fine with Annie. Clutching her gut, she made her way to the rows of seats and plunked herself down next to Travis who was sitting with his head tilted back and a pile of tissues pressed to this nose.

Annie's stomach hurt, but she wasn't sure if it was from the impact of the ball or the thought of now having to choose between the Halloween bout – which had been her idea – and slow-dancing in the arms of her dream guy.

71

She turned to Travis who smiled weakly from beneath his clump of tissues.

"I hate gym," he said.

"Hear, hear," sighed Annie.

As she watched the last few minutes of the sadistic ritual known as dodge ball, she made a mental list of pros and cons and weighed her options:

The bout was an important event for the Liberty Belles.

The dance was important, too, as a rite of passage for a teenager new to the United States.

The team *needed* her.

Tyler *wanted* her. At least as his date for that one evening … but if they hit it off who knew where that might lead?

There would be plenty of other bouts this season.

There would be only one Halloween dance.

She pictured herself bombing around the track as lead jammer, scoring points for the Liberty Belles.

She pictured herself cuddled up against Tyler, swaying to soft music.

Should she follow her heart? Or her conscience?

"*No?*" Tyler repeated the word back to her, as if she was speaking a foreign language.

"I'm sorry, Tyler," she said. "I would love to go with you, I just … can't."

They were standing outside the gymnasium. Tyler had surprised her after class, which was actually very sweet. He'd gone through the trouble of finding out which lesson she had so he could be waiting for her when she got out.

She had a feeling he wished he hadn't bothered.

When Annie had emerged from the gym, she'd spotted him immediately. Her first thought was that she should have spent more time fixing her hair after her disastrous dodge ball experience. She was probably all red in the face and still a little sweaty. Definitely not the way she wanted to look around Tyler.

"I don't understand," he was saying. "I thought you and I … I thought we … ya know … were kind of giving off vibes or whatever."

"Yes!" Annie nodded fast. "Yes, I thought that too. I mean, I still think that. It's just that I have another commitment on Saturday night."

"What's more important than the first dance of the school year?" Tyler asked curtly. He seemed less bewildered now, and more insulted.

Moment of truth. She hadn't admitted to being a roller girl the first time, but now she was determined to tell him. With a sigh, she reached into her backpack and pulled out a flyer for the Liberty Bells versus High Rollers Halloween bout.

"I'm a roller girl," she said, handing it to him.

"A what?"

"A roller girl. I'm on a roller derby team."

For a moment, he looked like he thought she might be joking.

"Seriously? Roller derby?" He shook his head. "Wow. I mean, I knew you hang out with those weirdos, but I just can't believe you play."

Annie ignored the implied insult and began to speak in a long, breathless rush. "I really love it and I don't want to let my team down. It's a proper sport. And it's really fun. Not just to play, but to watch. There's a great atmosphere and really cool music. I know the dance is a big deal, but I was kind of hoping that maybe you'd like to come and see me skate instead?"

Tyler looked at the flyer for a long moment. "I don't think that's really my scene." Then he stuffed the flyer in his back pocket, turned, and walked away.

Annie watched him go, feeling the tears prickling behind her eyes. Obviously, Tyler wasn't a boy who was used to being turned down. And by the new girl with the funny accent who played roller derby no less!

Again, the image of them dancing in each other's arms crossed her mind.

"What have I done?" Annie whispered. "What in the world have I done?"

Chapter Seven

That evening, Annie entered the rink with her skate bag slung over her shoulder and a scowl on her face.

Jesse looked up from where he was toying with the sound system and immediately did a double take. "Hey, who are you and what have you done with Annie?"

Annie snapped out of her mood just enough to ask, "Huh?"

"Well, you look like Annie, and you're wearing Annie's T-shirt, but the Annie I know usually shows up with a huge smile on her face. So who are you and what have you done with Anne R. Key?"

Annie sighed. "Sorry, Jesse. I guess I'm just not having a great day."

"Hmm." Jesse slid a CD into the player and hit a button.

"Maybe this'll help then."

Suddenly, the rink was filled with the sound of The Killers singing "Smile Like You Mean It".

This time, Annie did manage a smile. Jesse was so sweet. "Thanks. I love this song."

Annie made her way to the locker room, where the girls were all talking in low, concerned voices. The minute she entered, they stopped whispering and looked at her with sad eyes.

"Good news travels fast, I see," she said, slumping onto a bench.

"Well, yeah," Lauren admitted. "I mean, Tyler Erickson doesn't get turned down for a date every day."

"Tyler Erickson doesn't get turned down *any* day," Holly corrected. "Which is why you blowing him off for the dance is making headlines all over town."

"I didn't exactly blow him off," said Annie kicking off her shoes and tugging her skates out of her duffle bag. "I would have loved to have gone with him. It was a diary conflict."

The girls exchanged glances.

"Yeah, that's what we were talking about actually," said Liz.

"Look," said Lauren gently, "ultimately the decision is yours, but we kind of put it to a vote. Some of us say it would be totally fine if you decided to opt out of the bout to go to the dance with Tyler. And some of us say…"

"Some of us say that would be absolute garbage!" Holly piped up.

Annie had a pretty good idea which side Holly had voted on.

Sharmila gave Annie a hug. "Ordinarily, I'd say it would be dead wrong to skip a bout for a guy. But you're new here, and you've never been to a dance before."

"And Tyler's basically a god," Carmen added with a grin.

"True. And that made it even harder to tell him no. But it still isn't a good enough reason to miss the bout," Annie said.

"I know," said Carmen, looking sheepish. "Which is why I agree with Holly."

"It's great that you want to honour your commitment to your team," said Lauren. "We're just saying that this one time, it would be OK to miss the bout."

"I didn't say that," said Holly, in a surprisingly calm tone. "I said the exact opposite. I mean, I like cute guys as much as the next girl—"

"Maybe even *more* than the next girl," teased Liz, waggling her eyebrows.

"But life is full of tough choices, Princess. During the season, derby has to come first. Even if it means you won't be on the dance floor on Saturday night." She surprised Annie by giving her a hug. "But I just wanna say that I think it's pretty cool that you decided to skate."

"Right," said Sharmila. "But if you change your mind, just this once, that would be cool too."

"I missed a bout my first season," Liz said, giving Annie's shoulder a squeeze. "I was basically failing French, and there was a bout the night before my mid-term exam. If I didn't study I would have crashed and burned on the test. So I skipped the bout and stayed home to hit the books."

"That's different than a school dance," argued Carmen. "That's academics."

"All I'm saying is that things come up," Liz clarified.

"She needs to be loyal to the team."

"And the team needs to be loyal to her."

As her teammates debated, Annie's head swam. She knew it would be wrong to miss the bout, just like it would have been wrong to miss a gymnastics meet when she'd been competing at elite level. Other people were counting on her and she made a promise when she joined the team.

But her teammates – her *friends* – were telling her that given the special circumstances of the situation, they would understand if she chose the dance.

It was the nicest thing they could have said.

But she still wasn't going to do it. She loved derby and she loved these girls. And she totally respected Holly and Carmen for being honest with her.

"Hey!" she called to get their attention, then smiled around at the group. "Thanks, everyone. But the fact is I wouldn't miss our Halloween bout even if the *real* David Beckham asked me to the dance."

They all laughed and set about getting into their gear.

On their way out to the track, Sharmila gave her another hug. "One more thing," she said so that only Annie could hear. "If you guys are meant to be together, it will happen."

"I don't know," Annie said grimly. "He seemed pretty

darn annoyed."

Sharmila gave a dismissive wave. "That's how boys are. They pout. But trust me, if there's really something there, it will work out. And if it doesn't, it wasn't meant to be."

Annie smiled. It sounded like good advice. Of course, coming from Sharmila, it was probably slightly biased. What guy *wouldn't* give her a second chance?

"Let's go, girls," came Coach Ritter's voice across the rink.

Annie didn't have to be told twice. If there was one thing that was going to shake her out of her miserable mood, it was some high-powered derby action.

They spent some time warming up and doing drills, and then it was time for another scrimmage against the High Rollers.

"You're gonna get a little taste of what you can expect at the Halloween bout," Liz taunted. "And trust me, it's not gonna be candy."

"Why are you guys dressing as vampires?" the captain of the Rollers, Allison, shot back. "Because you suck?"

Everyone on both teams laughed at that one.

The bout began. The High Rollers took an early lead, but the Belles didn't let it throw them. They continued to skate at full throttle and keep their confidence high.

Holly made a great effort but didn't manage to score before the other team's jammer called off the first jam. Lauren, as pivot, was focused and determined, but the High Rollers had really brought it today. This was going to be a tough one to win.

It was Annie's turn to be jammer. By now, she had blown off some steam. She'd pushed the Tyler situation out of her mind. At that moment, the only thing she was thinking about was derby.

Then she turned to see that the other team's jammer was none other than Dee Stroyer.

"Heard you turned down Tyler for the Halloween dance," she scoffed. "Were you suffering from temporary insanity or are you always that stupid?"

"I'm not stupid." Annie gritted her teeth, trying not to let Dee's remark get to her. "I just have priorities," she said in an icy voice.

"Well, I hope you and your 'priorities' will be very happy together. I know Tyler and I will be when we're making out on the dance floor."

Annie's eyes flew open. "He asked you to the dance?"

"No, but since you turned him down, I might ask him. I've had my eye on him since the seventh grade. Even back then, word on the spin-the-bottle circuit was that he was the best kisser in town." Dee puckered up her lips and made exaggerated kissing noises.

Was it possible? Would Dee have the nerve to invite Tyler to the dance? And if she did, would he accept?

The whistle blew and Annie took off like a shot, skating in a fury. The idea of Tyler dancing with Dee – or anyone other than Annie herself – was infuriating. She tried to get the image out of her mind.

Unfortunately, she couldn't shake it.

She skated faster, determined to catch up with Dee. Dee seemed to sense her approach because she turned around and taunted her with another kissing sound.

Annie's anger ignited. She leaned forward and began running on her toe stops around a High Rollers blocker, then glided into some superfast crossovers.

The speed was exhilarating, and her movements were graceful and swift, but in her anger, she misjudged the turn, and lost her balance.

The world slipped out from under her and she went down hard.

Her left ankle took the brunt of it, twisting beneath her as she landed on it with all of her weight. A bolt of pain shot from her ankle like lightning.

Wincing, Annie tried to stand up, but her ankle wasn't having it.

With a groan, she crumbled back to the track.

Chapter Eight

The rest of the girls stopped skating and Coach Ritter hurried over.

"Give me your foot," she said gently. "Easy, easy…"

Gingerly, she removed Annie's skate.

"Ouch!" winced Annie. "Sorry, kiddo." Coach Ritter, who was also a registered nurse, lightly pressed her fingertips to Annie's ankle. "Can you move it?"

Annie attempted to wiggle her left ankle, but pain exploded all the way up her leg. She could see that her skin was already discolouring to a horrid purple and her ankle was beginning to swell.

"Is it broken?" Annie asked, her heart sinking.

"I don't think so," said Coach. "It looks more like a very bad sprain. But just to be on the safe side, I think you should have it X-rayed."

Annie felt a twinge of panic. "At the hospital?"

Coach smiled. "No, at the yogurt shop. Free soft serve with every CT scan!"

In spite of her pain and embarrassment, Annie laughed.

"That'a girl," said Coach. "I'm sure it's gonna be fine, but better safe than sorry, right?" She began unlacing Annie's right skate, then turned to the side of the track where Jesse was standing and called over to him. "Jesse, will you call an ambulance, please? And Annie's dad?"

Looking concerned, Jesse nodded and whipped out his phone. Then Liz and Lauren skated over to help Annie hobble off the track.

On her way, she made eye contact with Dee Stroyer.

Dee didn't even look sorry for goading her, which was the whole reason Annie had been so careless in the first place.

Still, it was Annie's own fault for letting anger cloud her judgment. She was the one who'd been skating like a reckless maniac.

As her teammates helped her to a bench, Annie's ankle continued to pound. It felt like it had swollen to ten times its normal size and it burned as though it were on fire.

And the worst part was that Annie had no one to blame but herself.

Correction: the *worst* part was that she wasn't going to be able to skate on it for days. Maybe even weeks. Even before the ambulance arrived, that much was obvious.

Carmen had run to the first-aid kit for a cold pack, and Sharmila had taken off her sweatshirt and bunched it up like a pillow so that Annie could lie back on the hard wooden bench.

"I sprained my wrist last year," said Holly. "It's pretty miserable at first but it'll calm down in a couple of hours. You've just gotta tough it out."

A moment later, the paramedics arrived and bundled Annie onto a stretcher.

The girls – Belles and Rollers alike – all wished her good luck. Dee Stroyer was the only one who said nothing.

The paramedics carefully transported her to the ambulance. Lauren clambered in after Annie, to hold her hand on the way to the hospital. Just before the doors closed, Jesse ran up.

Annie smiled weakly. "I crashed and burned, Jesse."

"Hey, there's a Savage Garden song called 'Crash and Burn'."

Annie laughed.

"Glad to see the pain hasn't affected your sense of humour," said Jesse with a smile.

"Did you get hold of my dad?"

"Yeah. He'll meet you at the ER." He met her eyes and held them. "Take it easy, OK, Annie?" he said softly. "You're gonna be fine."

Annie nodded. Then the doors closed and siren blared and she was off.

* * *

The ER wasn't very busy on a weekday afternoon. The first thing the receptionist had wanted to know was her insurance company. Annie had no idea what to tell her. Back in the UK, healthcare was free for everyone on the NHS. Hopefully Dad would be able to sort it out. In the waiting room Annie and Lauren struck up a conversation with a woman who'd suffered a deep cut in her thumb while slicing onions for a salad. The only other patient was a construction worker who'd fallen off a ladder and had a few minor bumps and bruises.

An older nurse, who introduced herself as Martha, helped Annie into a wheelchair and pushed her to a curtained partition at the end of the hall. Lauren came along, swinging Annie's skate bag.

"Are your folks on their way, hon?" Martha asked, making some notes on a chart in a file folder.

"My dad is," Annie replied. "He should be here soon."

Minutes later, a cute young doctor entered through the curtain.

"Hello, there. I'm Dr Borden." He cast an eye at Annie's swollen ankle and frowned. "If I had to guess, I'd say someone got hurt at cheerleading practice. Bad basket toss, perhaps?"

Annie had no idea what a basket toss was. "No, doctor," she replied. "I hurt myself in a roller derby scrimmage."

Martha looked up from Annie's file, intrigued. "Roller derby?"

Lauren nodded. "We're on a junior team in Liberty Heights."

"I didn't know we had roller derby in the area," said Martha, smiling. "When I was a little girl, my granddad used to take me to bouts in Chicago. Of course, that was years ago. But, oh, how I loved to watch those ladies skate!"

Dr Borden had taken Annie's foot in his hand and was carefully tipping it this way and that. Annie cringed as another stab of pain sliced through her.

"Sorry," said the doctor. "I know it hurts, but can you try and move it? Point your toes toward the ceiling."

Annie bit her lip and with a great effort managed to tip her foot upward. It throbbed but at least the movement proved that everything was still connected.

"That's good," said the doctor. "I'm going to send you off to radiology for a quick X-ray, but that's just me being cautious. I'd bet my stethoscope that it's just a really nasty sprain." He nodded to Martha who stepped out to make arrangements.

Dr Borden put his hands on his hips and grinned. "Roller derby, huh? My twins love to roller skate – they're only seven. Maybe they'd be interested some day."

"You should bring them to our Halloween bout!" said Annie. She motioned to Lauren to hand her the duffle bag and quickly fished out one of the flyers. "It's going to be great! We're wearing costumes and giving out sweets – I mean candy. And the bout itself is going to be pretty exciting. It's kind of a grudge match." She handed him the flyer.

"Thanks. Sounds like a lot of fun." He folded it neatly and tucked it into the pocket of his white coat, just as Annie's dad came skidding into the room. He looked frantic.

"Annie!" He crossed the room in two steps and threw his arms around her. "Are you all right?"

Dr Borden answered for her. "She's going to be fine," he said in a pleasant, confident tone. "I'm sending her for a little photo shoot down in radiology, but I suspect it will confirm what I've already told her. Nasty sprain, nothing more."

Annie took a deep breath and asked the question that had been worrying her since the minute she hit the rink. "When do you think I'll be able to skate again?"

"Well, Annie, that's hard to say. Off the top of my head I'm going to say about three weeks. But a lot will depend on you. If you follow my instructions and don't push yourself, it could be sooner. If you don't follow—"

"Oh, I will!" Annie blurted. "I'll do whatever you say. I just really want to be able to skate in the Halloween bout, and it's three weeks from Saturday."

"Slow down, Beanie," said Dad, holding up his palms. "Let's just see what happens."

"But, Dad!"

"I won't risk you doing any more damage to that ankle. You don't skate until the doctor clears you. Understood?"

Annie pouted, which made Dr Borden chuckle. "Your dad's right, Annie. If you skate before you're healed you can set your recovery back months. You wouldn't want that to happen, would you?"

"No, I suppose not." Annie sighed. "All right. I won't rush it."

"Good."

Martha returned, and helped Annie back into the wheelchair

for her ride to the radiology department. Lauren called her older brother for a ride home. Then she hugged Annie and told her to text her later to let her know what the X-ray showed.

"Here," said Lauren, handing the nurse another flyer for the Halloween bout. "Hope you can make it!"

"Thanks for coming with me," said Annie.

"You're my derby wife," said Lauren with a grin. "I know you'd be there for me, too."

Then Dr Borden walked Dad to the reception desk to fill out insurance forms and Martha rolled Annie away to have her "photo shoot".

"Cheer up, hon," Martha said, punching the lift button. "It could have been a lot worse."

"I know," said Annie.

As they rolled into the lift and the doors slid closed it occurred to Annie that the sprain really was the least of her problems; things *were* going to get worse.

A lot worse.

Because they still had to tell Mum!

Dad pulled his battered pickup out of the ER car park and into the early evening traffic.

Annie sat next to him, her bruised, swollen ankle encased in a clunky plastic boot.

"I've never been one of those girls who's mad for shoes," she said, "but I can tell you when it comes to fashionable footwear, this thing is definitely *not* in style."

"Look at the bright side," said Dad, snapping on the indicator. "You're halfway there if you decide to be Frankenstein for Halloween."

Annie would have laughed, but the mention of Frankenstein made her think of Jessica and her boyfriend, which made her think of the dance, which made her think of Tyler, which made her...

Miserable!

Dad stopped at a traffic light and reached over the driver's seat to hand Annie a sheet of paper.

"Dr Borden gave me this," he explained. "It describes what you need to do for the next few weeks."

Annie glanced at the neatly typed list. It went over the standard instructions for taking pain killers as needed and using crutches to get around. Then there was a section headed in bold capital letters: "RICE".

"So what does the good doctor prescribe?" asked Dad, turning left when the light changed to green.

"Rice," said Annie.

"Rice?" Dad frowned into the rear-view mirror. "Well, then maybe we should stop at Panda Garden on the way home. I wouldn't mind some General Tso's chicken."

"Not actual rice," grumbled Annie. Although a spring roll and some hot and sour soup sounded pretty good right then. "It's an acronym for Rest, Ice, Compression, and Elevation."

"Ah. Sounds effective." Dad shot her a grin in the mirror. "Although nowhere near as appetizing as General Tso's."

In spite of her mood, Annie laughed. "Fine, then. Panda Garden it is." She eyed the plastic boot. "But do you mind if we get takeaway? I really don't feel like stomping around in public in this hideous thing."

"Done and done," said Dad, turning in the direction of the Chinese restaurant.

The thought of a delicious meal cheered Annie somewhat. She loved Asian food, but for her, the best part was the fortune cookies. She closed her eyes and tried to imagine what wisdom the little white slip of paper might offer her tonight:

She who skates in anger fast, ends up in a plastic cast.

Annie was just finishing her second helping of vegetable fried rice when the doorbell rang.

"I'll get it," Dad said.

But Annie was already reaching for her crutches. "Let me," she said. "I've got to get used to these stupid things."

She adjusted the rubber tops of the crutches under her arms and began the slow, wobbly drag to the front door. When she opened it, she caught her breath.

Flowers! Lots of them, wrapped in pretty tissue and a big yellow bow.

And peeking out from behind the enormous bouquet were a

pair of familiar blue eyes.

"Jesse!"

"Hey, Annie." Jesse stepped into the hallway, handed her the flowers, and gave her a lopsided smile. "How's the ankle? What did the doctor say?"

"Bad sprain," she murmured, bringing the bouquet to her face and breathing deeply. "No big deal, except I'll be in this horrendous boot for two weeks."

"Oh, man." Jesse gave her a sympathetic look. "That really sucks. So you won't be able to skate?"

Annie shook her head and inhaled again. She'd never been given flowers from a boy before, and she had to admit, it was nice.

"Does it hurt?"

Annie was so busy admiring the cheerful mix of daisies, roses, and tulips that for a second she forgot all about the dull ache in her ankle. "Yes, but icing it helps a lot."

"Yeah. That'll keep the swelling down."

Dad appeared in the hallway, holding a takeaway carton. "Hi, Jesse!" When he spotted the gigantic bouquet, he looked almost as impressed as Annie. "Can I interest you in some crispy beef and broccoli?" he offered. "We've got plenty."

"No, thank you," said Jesse. "I've already eaten."

Dad's eyes went from Jesse to the flowers to Annie. He had a goofy grin on his face when he said, "Uh, I should probably go find a vase."

"Thanks, Dad." Annie already knew where she was going

to put them – on her bedside table where she could fall asleep admiring them and see them the minute she woke up in the morning. "Jesse, these are the most beautiful flowers I've ever seen. Thank you so much!"

"Uh, well—"

"You're really very sweet to think of this," she said softly. Annie was debating whether it would be weird to give him a kiss on the cheek. They were friends after all, and this was such a thoughtful gesture. Unfortunately, between her armful of flowers and her unwieldy crutches, there was really no graceful way to do it. If she leaned towards him she'd probably fall and sprain her other ankle. And maybe one of his in the bargain.

"You're welcome," said Jesse, looking uncomfortable. "But … they aren't exactly from me."

Annie blinked. "Huh?"

"The whole team chipped in for them. See?" He reached into his pocket and handed her a little rectangular card:

Get well, Anne R. Key! Love, Coach Ritter and the Liberty Belles

"I have to go by your street on my way home," Jesse explained awkwardly. "So I volunteered to drop them off."

"Oh." Annie wanted to curl up in a ball and disappear. *Why couldn't I have sprained my jaw instead?* she thought. *Then I wouldn't have been able to open my mouth and humiliate myself.* She was sure her face was pinker than Holly's favourite fishnets. "Well, that was nice of you. I appreciate it."

"No problem."

They stood there, with Annie feeling like a colossal idiot, for what seemed like a thousand years.

"I, um, I guess I should, er, get these into some water," Annie stammered at last.

"Right," said Jesse. "Well, take it easy on that ankle. I'll see you in school tomorrow."

And then, to Annie's great relief, he left.

Dad returned with the vase just as the door closed behind Jesse. He was just opening his mouth to comment, but Annie spoke first.

"They're not from him. They're from the Belles."

"Oh." Dad looked genuinely disappointed. "Well, then I guess I can call Westminster Abbey and tell them we *won't* be needing that date I just booked for your wedding?"

Annie laughed in spite of herself. "Yeah. Tell them my engagement's off, so if Prince Harry's looking for a girlfriend, I'm still totally available."

"Not a chance," said Dad, taking the bouquet so that Annie could hobble back towards the kitchen. "If you married a prince you'd have to move back to England and I'd miss you way too much." Then he planted a loud kiss on top of her head as she wobbled past him. "Speaking of England," he continued, "I'm going to call your mum now and let her know what happened."

"No!" Annie cried out. She knew Mum would somehow blame Dad for Annie's injury. She didn't want to subject him to the inevitable argument. "I'll call her myself."

"Well, don't put it off – she's your mother and she deserves to know," Dad said, giving her a serious look.

"I'll tell her," Annie promised.

But not tonight. She'd had more than enough drama for one day.

Chapter Nine

The next few days were a challenge on several fronts.

The discomfort in her ankle kept Annie awake most of the night since every little twist or turn made the injury ache. And although Annie wasn't exactly a fashionista, the ugly grey plastic boot clashed with pretty much everything in her wardrobe. As far as accessories went, crutches were the worst. After five days of use, the skin under her arms was rubbed raw from leaning on her crutches.

The good news was that she wasn't in it alone. In addition to Lexie, every Liberty Belle who attended Liberty Heights High made it her business to be available to help Annie get around school with as little difficulty as possible.

"You know I only volunteered to help you hobble around

because it gets me out of class five minutes early, right?" Lexie's hazel eyes sparkled as she stuffed Annie's backpack into the locker and dug around for *Wuthering Heights.*

"Oh, I know." Annie leaned on her crutches and smiled. "In fact, the whole reason I injured myself was so that you could skip out of classes early."

Lexie laughed. "That's what I call a true friend. And if you ever need me to break an arm or crack a rib on your behalf, I'll be happy to do it."

Annie shook her head. "Don't even joke about that," she said in a serious voice. "This may only be a sprain but it hurts like crazy. Not to mention all the inconvenience."

"Speaking of that," said Lexie with a sly grin. "Here comes your next escort, right on schedule."

Annie turned to see Jesse walking down the empty corridor. She felt a wave of embarrassment remembering the whole awkward flower incident, but it didn't last. He was her friend, and silly things like that didn't matter between friends. She couldn't help but notice how cool he looked in a faded Dead Kennedys T-shirt. His eyes were the same blue as the distressed denim of his baggy jeans.

"Inconvenience never looked so good, huh?" teased Lexie.

"Stop it," Annie whispered, a faint blush on her cheeks. "It's only Jesse."

Lexie gave a slow, appreciative nod. "Yes, it is."

"Lex! Cut it out. He's just a friend."

"Right." Lexie rolled her eyes. "Whatever."

Jesse arrived and gave them a solemn look. "I just want you to know that I'm missing the first five minutes of a very important lecture on the trade policies of the Roosevelt era," he announced in a serious voice. Then he flashed a huge smile at Annie. "So basically, I owe you big time!"

Lexie giggled and handed him Annie's English notebook and the Brontë novel. Then she flounced off to catch up with a few of her arty friends from manga club before her first class.

Annie felt even clumsier than usual, planting and hopping her way down the hall beside Jesse. The rubber tips of her crutches squeaked on the polished floors.

"You haven't been around the rink much," Jesse observed, holding the door at the end of the hall open and waiting for her to hobble through.

"What would be the point?" Annie said, sighing. "I can't skate."

"No, but you could still take part. You could ref scrimmages, or keep score, or just cheer your teammates on."

Annie stopped hobbling and looked at him. It had never occurred to her to show up at the rink and watch practice. Instead, she'd been sitting home on the sofa, icing her ankle, and sulking.

"You're absolutely right, Jess. I suppose I thought it would be too depressing to be there and not be able to skate, but it sounds like I could actually be useful." She shook her head. "I'm such an idiot for not realizing it myself."

They arrived at her English classroom just as the class bell rang. Annie pressed herself against the lockers while a flood of students gushed into the hall. When the room was empty, she hopped inside and went to her desk. Jesse followed, placing her books on the desk, then holding her crutches while she arranged herself in the seat. Her booted foot stuck out in the aisle, but there was really nowhere else for her to put it.

Jesse went to prop the crutches against the back wall of the room. Then, to Annie's surprise, he came back and sat facing her on top of the desk in front.

Tyler's desk.

"I hope I didn't sound like a jerk about you missing practice," he said, looking guilty. "I just thought it would be better for you to be there, keeping busy, than home all alone. Besides, the team really misses you." He paused. "And, ya know … I guess *I*—"

"Dude. You're on my desk."

Annie looked up to see Tyler standing behind Jesse, and he didn't look happy. Annie hadn't even noticed him come in. Strange, as usually she was aware of his presence the minute he came within ten metres of her, like she had some sort of built-in tracking device.

But just now, she'd been too involved in what Jesse had been saying.

And what *had* Jesse been saying? That her teammates missed her. And that *he* … He *what*?

"Go ahead, Jesse," she blurted out. "Finish what you were going to say."

"It was nothing," said Jesse, shaking his head and sliding off the desk. Then he stepped aside so that Tyler could take his seat.

Tyler stepped carefully over Annie's boot and put his books on the desk. Actually, he kind of slammed them down. He gave Jesse a sharp look, then turned his back to Annie and slid into the chair.

"So should I come back at the end of the period?" Jesse asked. "Or is there someone in this class who can carry your books for you?"

Tyler turned around to face Annie and looked like he was about to say something, but Annie had already started to reply. "Thanks, but Tessa will help me get to history."

Tyler frowned slightly and faced the front again.

"Tessa the Distress-a." Jesse grinned. "OK. So if I don't see you later, then I'll see you at the rink."

"See ya there!" Annie assured him as he made his way to the door. She was actually looking forward to showing up for practice today, even if she couldn't skate. Maybe she could be the timekeeper, or even do some light stretching.

Her happy thoughts were interrupted by a sweet voice from the row next to her.

"I've been meaning to ask you," drawled Kelsey, "how did you get hurt?"

Annie really didn't want to have a conversation with her nemesis, but since it would have been rude not to answer she tersely said, "I fell."

"Not for that skater guy, I hope," said Kelsey, pretending to misunderstand. "I mean, HELLO ... did you see that shirt he was wearing?"

"No, I actually fell. At roller derby practice," Annie explained.

"Roller derby, right. Brutal bruisers on roller skates. Now I remember."

"It's not brutal," said Annie. "It requires a lot of coordination and skill."

"Which," said Kelsey, pointedly eyeing Annie's cast, "you obviously don't have, or you wouldn't be clomping around in that ugly boot." She sighed. "Well, Annie, I'm just glad you found a sport that suits you. Personally, I never thought you were right for cheerleading anyway." She gave her glossy blonde hair a toss.

"Kelsey—" Tyler said in a warning voice.

But before Tyler could finish what he was about to say, Ms Schwarz told them to open their books, and class began.

Annie's plan to go to the rink after school met one very stubborn obstacle.

Transport.

Usually she skated to the rink, but for obvious reasons, that was out of the question. All the extra Halloween baking Dad had to do meant that he would still be working in the shop long after closing time, and Annie hadn't arranged to get a lift from any of the other Belles.

At the last minute, she called Liz, who was a senior and had her own car. Liz said she'd be happy to drive Annie any other time, but today just didn't work. She had a dentist appointment right before practice and wouldn't have time to double back to pick up Annie before heading to the rink.

"I'll drive you on Thursday, though," Liz had promised.

Once again, this left Annie alone on the couch with an ice pack on her ankle and a rerun of *I Love Lucy* on the TV. Annie sighed in frustration. She was still struggling to get used to how dependent Americans were on cars. Back in London, she'd hardly ever travelled by car – there was no need, with regular buses and Underground trains to whisk her across town. But in Liberty Heights there was next to no public transport and big distances between places. Annie was beginning to understand why American teens couldn't wait to get their driving licence.

Ironically, last night her flyer on the café bulletin board had finally yielded a result: she'd got her first call for a babysitting job, but had to turn it down due to her injury. The lady on the other end of the phone had sounded disappointed, but promised to call again in the future.

The house felt so empty. What it lacked in current décor, it made up for in size, and Annie felt completely abandoned in the large space. She was so lonely, in fact, that she found herself desperately wishing that her mum was there.

Not that Philippa had ever been a cuddly, affectionate sort of mother, but at least she would be company.

Annie brightened, realizing that that maybe Mum *could* keep her company!

She grabbed her crutches and headed to the kitchen where

she'd left her laptop. Seconds later, the machine was beeping musically, Skyping Annie's mother in England.

"Annie, love!" Mum's voice preceded her video image by a half a second. When her face appeared, Annie could see that she was still in her office. There were takeaway food containers on her otherwise impeccably tidy desk. In London it was after eleven in the evening.

"Hi, Mum. How are you?"

"Busy. Big case, you know."

Annie resisted the urge to say, "What else is new?"

"I'm sure you'll win it," she replied instead.

Mum smiled. "How are you doing over there? School good? Making friends?"

"Fine, it's OK, and yes." Annie laughed but she felt a tiny prickle of anger that Mum didn't ask about Dad. Even if it was just to be polite, she could have enquired.

"I have to tell you something," Annie began. "Better yet, I'll show you…" Annie tilted the computer screen and gingerly lifted her booted foot. "*Ta da!* Lovely, isn't it?" She motioned gracefully to the ugly cast, pretending to be modelling it. "It's what all the trendy injured girls are wearing this season! Goes with everything. Except stairs. And roller skates." She laughed, but even to her it sounded forced.

On the screen, Mum's face had gone pale. "You broke your leg?" she cried.

"I sprained my ankle," she corrected, "which is a total downgrade from a broken leg. And I did it at derby practice."

"When?"

Annie hesitated. She knew her mother would be furious when Annie told her the fall had happened five days ago. Annie considered fibbing, but as a lawyer, her mother sniffed out liars for a living. There would be no putting one over on Philippa Bradley QC.

"Five days ago," she admitted.

Mum's eyes narrowed and she banged her fist on her desk. This caused her cardboard takeaway cup of tea to topple, spilling liquid all over the documents she had spread across the desktop.

Great.

Furious, Mum began mopping up the spill. "Why didn't your father tell me immediately?" she demanded. "He should have called me the instant it happened."

"Why?" said Annie in a frosty voice. "Would you have hopped on the first flight out of Heathrow and flown over here to hold my hand?"

Mum's head snapped up from the sopping papers. When her eyes met Annie's on the screen it occurred to Annie that they were looking at one another across thousands of miles – both literally and figuratively.

Mum, to her credit, didn't say, "Of course I would have," because they both knew that would have been a lie. "I should have been told," she said feebly. "I love you, Annie. Naturally I'd want to know if you'd been hurt."

"Dad told me to call you," Annie confessed. "I just didn't have the guts. I knew what you were going to say."

"Did you?" Mum gave up on the ruined paperwork and sat back in her desk chair, folding her arms across her chest. "Did you know that I would say I absolutely hate the thought of you taking part in such a dangerous sport?"

"Gymnastics is dangerous," Annie reminded her. "Girls get seriously hurt all the time."

"That's different," said Mum. "You were *trained* in gymnastics, so you knew how to protect yourself. And your coaches were among the best in the country. Who, may I ask, coaches this roller derby squad of yours? Some toothless ex-convict?"

Annie gasped. "Mum, that's a horrible thing to say!"

Mum looked contrite. "I'm sorry, Annie. I suppose I don't know much about this derby sport, but the stereotypes I'm familiar with—"

"Are stereotypes and nothing more!" Annie snapped. "My coach happens to be a wonderful woman. She's athletic and smart, and she's a registered nurse. In fact, *she* works night shifts so *she* can be at home with her kids."

Annie felt guilty the moment she said it, but remarkably, Philippa didn't comment on the insult. "Be that as it may," said Mum, "I think you should stop playing this game."

Annie felt as though someone had kicked her in the stomach. "What?"

"It's too risky. Do you realize how lucky you are that it was just a sprain?"

Annie frowned at the screen, and Mum let out a long sigh.

"I'm going to speak to your father about it," she said. "I mean, really, allowing his daughter to play a contact sport… Where was he when you were being pummelled? Icing cupcakes?"

Annie's jaw tightened; it was all she could do to keep from clicking the "end call" button, which in essence would have been hanging up on her own mother. Instead, she smiled into the tiny camera. "As a matter of fact, he was. Icing cupcakes, brewing tea, and counting money! He's very, very busy. Rosie Lee's is a huge success!"

Mum lifted an eyebrow sceptically. "Is that so?"

"Yes! It's the most popular place in town."

"The most popular place in Liberty Heights, Illinois?" Mum rolled her eyes and gave a condescending chuckle. "The point is, your father has no common sense whatsoever, and the fact that he's agreed to let you play roller derby is just further proof of it."

That was it. Annie couldn't take any more. "Gotta go, Mum," she said.

"What?" Mum looked surprised. "Why?"

"Well, you know us roller derby girls," said Annie. "I've got a meeting with my parole officer."

Mum's mouth dropped opened, but before she could scold Annie for being snarky, Annie ended the Skype call.

It wasn't until the screen was blank and she'd closed the computer that her tears began to fall. How could her mum be so unkind? So self-important and judgmental?

As she limped back to the living room, Annie felt a stab of pain. But it wasn't her ankle – it was the realization that any fantasies she'd been harbouring about her parents getting back together had just been blown to bits.

Annie visited Dr Borden on Friday afternoon and was told that the swelling in her ankle had gone down enough that she could remove the boot. It was still too sore to walk on, though, so she'd be relying on the crutches a bit longer.

"What about the Halloween bout?" she asked, her voice so hopeful it almost sounded desperate.

Dr Borden frowned. "Still can't say for sure. It looks promising, but I don't want to make a definite decision just yet. We'll have another look at in a week."

Annie decided to take a glass-half-full approach and consider that good news. After all, he hadn't said no.

"By the way," said Dr Borden, as Annie's dad handed her the crutches. "I told my kids about the bout. They can't wait to go!"

"That's great!" said Annie. "I'll save them some extra pieces of candy."

"Better not do that," said the doctor, winking. "My wife's a dentist!"

In the corridor, Annie waved to the nurse, Martha. "Coming to the bout?"

"Wouldn't miss it!"

"Sounds like this is shaping up to be a real event," Dad observed as they exited the emergency room.

"Yeah," said Annie, struggling to remain optimistic. "I only hope I'll get to be a part of it."

Chapter Ten

The next morning, Dad woke Annie early to help him bake more Halloween treats. As Lexie had predicted, many people in the neighbourhood had begun placing orders for baked goodies to serve at their costume parties and post-trick-or-treating get togethers. Word of Dad's talents had spread and business was beginning to pick up.

Lexie had also come over to Rosie Lee's and was using washable paints to decorate the shop windows with ghosts, goblins, and skeletons.

Finally, Dad slid the last batch of cupcakes into the oven and took off his apron.

"Those are the last two dozen," he announced. "Mrs Helmsford will be in to pick them up at noon. She wants them frosted to look like miniature mummy heads." He gave Annie a sideways glance. "And speaking of mummies … I spoke to your mother last night."

Annie cringed. She'd been expecting this conversation.

"She tells me you were snippy with her when you Skyped."

There was no point in denying it, so Annie just shrugged. "Guilty as charged," she said with a sigh.

"Look, Beanie. I know things are complicated between Mum and me, but she's your mother. And that means you treat her with respect."

"OK," said Annie, nodding. Then she drew a deep breath. "Did she tell you she wants me to quit derby?"

At the window, Lexie stopped painting and turned to gape at Annie. "You didn't tell me she said that!"

"I was trying to pretend she hadn't," said Annie. "Well, Dad? Did she tell you I had to quit?"

Dad, who was wiping chocolate batter off his hands, cleared his throat. "She may have mentioned something to that effect, yes."

"And what did you say?"

"Well, I told her I felt the same way she did at first. Then I casually suggested that if you did quit derby, you might give cheerleading a try."

"What?!" said Lexie.

Annie was equally shocked. "Dad! I would never."

Dad grinned. "Well, I know that. And you know that. But Mum doesn't know that. Then I described to her the way the

Liberty Heights High cheerleaders build those enormous human pyramids and then do backflips off of one another's shoulders or get flung up into the air."

Annie laughed. "You didn't!"

"Sure I did. And I think she got the picture." He raised his eyebrows and put on a Transylvanian accent. "Danger is lurking every-vare, no matter vut sport you choose!"

Lexie laughed. "Good for you, Mr Turner."

"That's Count Dracula to you, missy!"

"Maybe I should design a costume for you, too."

But Dad shook his head. "Thanks anyway, Lexie, but I've already got one." He reached under the counter and pulled out a shopping bag. "I picked these up yesterday."

"These?" Annie felt a little twinge of worry. "That's plural."

"Yes, it is. And I'm glad to see you're learning something in high school."

"Dad, what's in the bag?"

In reply, he pulled out an intensely hairy werewolf mask and slipped it over his head.

"Oh, wow!" Lexie cracked up. "Aren't there rules in the food-service industry? I think you'd better get a hairnet ... fast!"

"The sad part," giggled Annie, trying to smooth down the tangle of hair that stuck out all around the mask, "is that this isn't really all that much worse than his normal hair!"

"She's got a point," said Dad, his voice muffled inside the rubber head. "I do kind of like the fangs, though, don't you?"

"All the better to eat gingerbread skeletons with!" joked Annie.

Then Dad pulled a second costume out of the bag. "I got this for you," he said, handing her a black conical hat.

"Dad, really?" Annie sighed, remembering his brilliant idea to dress her up as Queen Elizabeth II for the grand opening of Rosie Lee's. "Again?"

"This is entirely different. This time you'll be a very funky witch. Our beloved queen is *not* a witch!"

"She's not particularly funky, either," Lexie observed.

Then Dad produced a stack of flyers he'd printed out.

COME TO ROSIE LEE'S AND SIT FOR A "SPELL" YOU WON'T KNOW "WITCH" OF OUR TASTY TREATS YOU'LL WANT TO BE "GOBLIN" UP FIRST!

"Do I really have to?" Annie grumbled, eyeing the costume. She had to admit it was a major improvement over the frumpy queen outfit – it was a little black velvet minidress with flowing lace sleeves. The hat, on closer inspection, was dotted all over with colourful little jewels and the tights were pink and green neon stripes. Still, she'd much rather hand out the ads dressed in jeans and a jacket.

Dad, concealed behind the werewolf mask, began to whimper like a hurt puppy.

"Aw, c'mon, Annie," said Lexie, biting back a grin. "How can you say no to that?"

"Fine," huffed Annie. "I'll do it." She looked at the stack of flyers and inspiration struck. "As long as you let me hand out the

Liberty Belles flyers at the same time."

"I can live with that," said Dad, lifting the mask and giving her a smile.

Minutes later, Annie emerged from the little office behind the kitchen wearing the crazy tights, dress, and hat.

"That's actually pretty cute," said Lexie.

Annie checked her reflection in the glass of the pastry display case and was pleased to see that Lexie was telling the truth. But she still wasn't thrilled about parading up and down Main Street in costume, no matter how well the dress showed off her legs. Her ankle was well enough that she could manage on one crutch and carry the flyers – Dad's and hers – in her other hand.

"Well, 'witch' me luck," she said, heading for the door.

For the next twenty minutes, she stood on the pavement outside Rosie Lee's feeling like an absolute idiot. Two grade-school boys rode by on bikes and laughed at her.

"Don't you know Halloween isn't for two more weeks?" scoffed one.

"Oh, shut up or I'll turn you both into toads!" hissed Annie.

The boy stuck his tongue out and they rode off, laughing.

Annie approached a sweet-looking elderly couple who were out for a walk. "Hello there!" she said, handing them a flyer. "You two look like you might enjoy a freshly baked cake and a cup of tea."

"Sounds delightful," said the old woman.

Annie opened the door for the couple and they ambled into the shop. She could hear them exclaiming over the delicious aromas as the door swung closed behind them.

When she turned back to scan the foot traffic on the pavement a familiar face caught her eye.

"Coach Ritter!" she called, waving madly.

The coach was holding the hands of two of the most adorable little kids Annie had ever seen.

"Annie, how nice to see you."

"Mommy!" cried the older one, a girl, ducking behind her mother. "She's a witch!"

Coach laughed. "Don't be silly, Abigail. It's only a costume. There's no such thing as witches."

"Your mum is right," said Annie, giving little Abigail a big smile. "I'm not a witch, but I am … a roller girl!"

Abigail's big green eyes lit up. "For real?"

"This little guy is Brandon," said Coach Ritter. "Abbey, Brandon, this is my friend Annie. Say hello."

"Hello."

"Hehwo."

Annie giggled. "They're so cute!"

"Thanks." Coach smiled fondly at her two children and tousled their ginger hair. "They're also quite a handful. We've been shopping all morning, and I'm exhausted."

"You know what you could do with, don't you?" said Annie, grinning.

"You mean besides a nanny?"

"How does a nice hot cup of pumpkin spiced tea and a cinnamon apple muffin sound?"

Coach smiled. "It sounds incredible."

"Then follow me!" Annie led her coach straight to the door of Rosie Lee's.

Inside, Coach helped the kids off with their jackets and hung them on coat pegs; she lingered there, her eyes flicking over the notices on the bulletin board while Brandon and Abbey ran straight for the pastry display.

"Mommy, can I have a cookie?" cried Abbey.

"Cupcake!" said Brandon.

Unfortunately, Dad picked that moment to come out from behind the counter wearing his werewolf mask. Abbey let out a terrified yelp, then ran shrieking to hide behind her mother.

"I'm sorry!" said Dad, quickly tugging off the scary rubber head. "Look, look, it's only a mask, sweetie. I'm not a monster, I'm just a person!"

Abbey peeked out from behind Coach Ritter, sniffling, but still didn't make a move to come out from her hiding place.

Brandon, on the other hand, went directly up to Annie's dad and kicked him soundly in the shin. "You fwightened my sistuh!"

Dad yelped, just like Abbey had.

"Brandon!" cried Coach Ritter, clearly mortified. "That wasn't nice."

"It's all right," said Dad, smiling as he rubbed his lower leg. "He was just protecting his big sister. I'm actually very impressed with his heroism."

"Me too," said Lexie, offering Brandon a high five. "Way to go, little guy."

"Around here, we reward heroes with gingerbread skeletons," said Annie, limping around to the back of the counter. She took two warm cookies off a baking sheet and brought them out to Brandon and Abigail.

"For the brave hero and the damsel in distress," she announced, sweeping an elegant bow to each of the children.

"Thank you," said Brandon, taking his cookie and chomping off the skeleton's head.

Abbey giggled, then took a bite of her cookie, too.

By now, the elderly couple Annie had coaxed into the shop had finished their refreshments and were making their way to the door.

"Hope you enjoyed everything, folks," said Dad, waving. "Please come again."

"Oh, you can count on it," said the old man.

"The cookies were delicious," his wife added, patting little Brandon on his head as she passed, then pointing to Dad's shin. "But we especially liked the exciting floor show."

When they were gone, Annie, Lexie, Dad, and Coach Ritter burst out laughing.

After adjusting her glitzy pointed hat, Annie left Coach and her kids to enjoy their cookies and tea and headed back outside. She handed out flyers for Rosie Lee's to everyone she saw – but she was far more selective about who she "invited" to the bout.

Families with energetic young kids definitely got the derby flyer, as did tweens and teens who looked sporty, or artsy and creative. Snobby-looking women or girls in designer clothes yapping on mobile phones did *not* get the nod. Neither did suited business men. Annie wondered if she was being just as bad as Mum in reacting to stereotypes, but she couldn't waste the bout flyers on anyone who seemed stuffy, or overly conservative.

Dad had been right about the witch costume, though. Most people were already in the Halloween spirit and when they stopped to admire her spooky-cute look, they couldn't help but notice Rosie Lee's. And since the day was crisp and cool, a good amount went in for a takeaway cup of tea or coffee. The jangling of the little silver bell on the shop door made pleasant background music for Annie as she schmoozed with shoppers.

During the lulls in people passing she'd go to the café windows and annoy Lexie, who was still painting them from the other side, by making faces and doing silly little dances on her one good foot.

Lexie had finished her goblins and was now painting a cemetery scene on the large main window. A tombstone for the dear departed (and fictional) Rosie Lee was the centrepiece of the mini-mural and the headline (which had been Annie's idea) read "Our Baked Goods are to Die For".

Annie stood at the window and pressed her nose to the glass, which made Coach Ritter's kids crack up.

Strange that they had stayed so long, Annie thought. Coach was on her second cup of coffee and the kids had graduated from cookies to cupcakes. There were no customers waiting to be served, so Dad, ever the gracious host, had sat down at the table with Coach Ritter and they seemed to be having a lively chat.

"Love the raven!" said Annie, pointing to the big black

bird Lexie had painted in the upper corner of the window. She danced around, flapping her arms like a bird and making squawking noises.

"Oh. My. God."

Annie froze. The voice was unmistakable. And it was right behind her.

She turned slowly and came face to face with Kelsey, whose expression was a mixture of amusement and disgust.

But that wasn't even the most humiliating part of the situation.

Kelsey wasn't by herself, or even just flanked by her two usual sidekicks.

She was standing there staring at Annie with half the cheerleading squad and at least eight soccer players.

One of whom was Tyler.

"This is absolutely pathetic," said Kelsey to the sidekick on her left, Ginger. "She's so desperate for attention she's dressing up in costume and dancing on the street."

"Pathetic," said Ginger with a smirk.

"At least she's dressed appropriately," noted Lulu, sidekick number two.

Kelsey gave Annie a long once over. "True. I mean, she is a total witch … give or take a letter."

Kelsey reached out and snatched one of the derby flyers from Annie. Without even glancing at it, she crumpled it up and tossed it to Tyler.

"Cut it out, Kelsey," he grumbled, stuffing the flyer into his pocket.

Annie wasn't sure if he was just embarrassed by Kelsey's rudeness, or if he was actually defending Annie.

Just go, Annie willed silently. *Take your nasty little popular clique and be on your way.*

With a flick of her hair, Kelsey started walking. But luck was not on Annie's side today. At that moment, Dad, still sporting his stupid mask, pushed open the café door and let out a long, wolfish howl.

"Hey there, boys and ghouls!" he called. "Anybody hungry?"

One of the soccer players, Javier, had approached the window and was gazing across the shop at the goodies in the display case. "I could use some carbs," he said. "Those chocolate chip cookies look pretty awesome."

"They are," Dad assured him. "Just ask Annie. I'm her dad."

Annie gulped.

A few of the soccer players remembered their manners and said hello.

"I wouldn't mind a hit of caffeine," said the goalie, Jackson. "How's the coffee in this place?"

"Best in town," said Dad. "And for Annie's friends, the first cup is always on the house. C'mon in, kids."

"That's great!" chirped Kelsey, beaming at Dad, then lowered her voice to hiss, "Too bad we aren't her friends."

Annie watched in horror as the entire popular crowd filed into Rosie Lee's, just as Coach Ritter and her kids were finally leaving. The last person through the door was Tyler. He paused to glance over his shoulder at Annie, but his expression was unreadable.

Lexie, who'd watched the entire disaster through the window, was shaking her head in sympathy as she waved Annie inside.

Annie would have much rather taken off and ran as far away from Rosie Lee's as possible, maybe even all the way back to England (including swimming across the Atlantic). But her ankle prohibited her from running as far as her own house.

So, having nothing else to do, she limped her way to the door of the café and followed the cool crowd inside.

The boys couldn't seem to get enough of Dad's baked goods. Javier alone ate three chocolate chip cookies, two blood clot brownies, and a gingerbread skeleton.

Kelsey, however, absolutely forbade her cheerleaders from so much as tasting anything. "Can you say 'carb overload'?" she sneered.

The girls obediently ordered black coffee and nothing else.

Tyler had a peanut butter cookie, but didn't say much.

By now, Dad had shed the mask and had pulled up a chair so that he was actually sitting with the soccer players, telling them stories about the English Premier League. The boys actually seemed to be enjoying Dad's company as much as they were enjoying his baked goods. There was a heated debate over whether Manchester United would win the league this year, and a philosophical discussion as to why Major League Soccer still wasn't a dominant force in the American sports world.

Annie wished the ground would open up and swallow her.

When Javier pointed out the "awesome mural", on the wall, Dad proudly announced that the artist just happened to be present and pointed to Lexie with a grand flourish.

For a second, Annie feared that Lexie might impale Dad with a paintbrush. But when Javier crossed the room to admire the painting up close, and asked her why she'd neglected to include Mick Jagger in the bus, Lexie blushed a little.

"I would have loved to paint Mick," she admitted. "But I ran out of room."

That was the only encouragement Dad needed; he launched into a story about a Rolling Stones concert he attended in London in the early nineties.

Annie kept herself busy behind the counter, filling orders for the walk-ins and occasionally hobbling over to deliver another cookie or cupcake to one of the soccer players.

On one of these trips, she accidentally made eye contact with Tyler again.

He looked as though he wanted to say something, but before he could, Kelsey popped up from her seat.

"We should go," she said. It wasn't a suggestion, it was an order, and her minions knew it. They stood up immediately. The soccer players seemed a little more reluctant to leave, but they got to their feet too.

"Thanks, Mr Turner," said Javier, shaking Dad's hand. "You can bet we'll be back."

To Annie's shock, Tyler spoke up next. "You might want to think about running a tab for this guy," he advised, smiling amiably at her dad. Then, for the briefest of seconds, he turned the smile to Annie.

"Sounds good to me," said Dad. "Maybe I'll even send a batch of those blood clot brownies to the Halloween dance for the snacks table."

Tyler's smile vanished abruptly and Annie felt her heart flip inside her chest.

Why did Dad have to bring up the dance?

The other boys thanked Dad, and, surprisingly, so did a few of the girls.

Then, when the "cool kids" were finally gone, Annie collapsed into a chair.

"Well, that was nice," said Dad. Completely oblivious to Annie's discomfort, he went back into the kitchen.

Nice? Annie thought. Was he serious?

She'd spent the last half an hour being silently judged by Kelsey and basically ignored by Tyler.

So in Annie's mind, the experience had fallen somewhere between miserable and humiliating. As far as she was concerned, the only *nice* thing about that visit was that it was over.

Chapter Eleven

To Annie, it felt like coming home.

The sound of the skates on the track, the feel of the cool air in the soaring space, and the smell of ... well, maybe it would be better not to dwell too much on the smell in the roller rink, which was a less-than-fresh blend of old carpet, sweaty skaters, and burned popcorn.

And fantastically familiar.

Annie stood on the threshold and smiled at the scene before her.

The music was loud, just the way she liked it. Jesse was at his usual post, tinkering with the wheel beds on the rental skates, Liz was leading the Liberty Belles in their pre-skate stretching routine, and Coach Ritter was making sure the girls were giving it their all.

Lauren was the first one to notice Annie and let out a cry of delight. In the next second, Annie was being mobbed by her teammates, crushed in a wonderfully welcoming group hug.

"Hey, hop-along," Holly joked. "It's about time you showed your face around here."

"I agree," said Coach, smiling and handing Annie a stopwatch. "As long as you're out of commission, I can use an assistant coach."

"I accept," said Annie, touched by the warm reception.

Then Coach blew her whistle and the team headed for the track. Coach hung back to accommodate the slow progress of Annie's one-crutch gait.

"So how's it feeling?" Coach asked, indicating the ankle. "Healing well?"

"You tell me," said Annie, lowering herself to a nearby bench and hiking up the leg of her jeans.

Like a superhero shifting identity, Coach Ritter became Nurse Ritter and began a careful examination of Annie's ankle. Annie was pleased to note that there was hardly any pain when her coach pressed her fingers around the bone.

"It's actually looking really good," said Coach Ritter. "The bruising isn't as bad as it was and it's barely swollen at all."

Annie felt a rush of hope. "Do you think I'll be able to skate soon?"

"Well..." Coach smiled. "Soon is kind of a vague term, but yes, I think so."

"In time for the Halloween bout?" Annie pressed.

"I want that as much as you do, kiddo. But I really wouldn't presume to say. That's up to your doctor."

Annie frowned. "I was afraid you were going to say that."

Coach gave her a sympathetic look. "I'd say 'be patient', but I'm talking to a teenager and I know that patience isn't in the teen repertoire." She laughed and helped Annie up from the bench. "Now c'mon, let's make these Belles do some drills. You're my official timer."

As they headed for the track, Coach paused. "And by the way, I really had a great time at Rosie Lee's the other day."

Annie beamed. "I'm glad to hear that. The food really is great, isn't it?"

"Yes. And your dad is a terrific guy. He's got a great sense of humour."

"Oh. Well, yeah, sure…" Was it Annie's imagination or was her roller derby coach *blushing?* "Dad's the best."

"He showed me your babysitting ad," said Coach, smiling. "Are you free to babysit my two monsters tomorrow night for a few hours?"

"I'd love to!" Annie replied. Brandon and Abbey were adorable. *Looking after them will be a piece of cake*, Annie thought.

"Great! I'll pick you up at seven," Coach said.

Then she blew her whistle and the Belles began their drills. Annie tried to stay focused on the timing but Coach's blush kept distracting her. Was she reading too much into it?

After several minutes of serious skating, Coach called for a break and went to find Slammy Tammy, the High Rollers' coach, to arrange an impromptu scrimmage.

Annie joined her teammates, who were huddled at the side of the rink, drinking from their water bottles.

"It's not the same without you on the track," said Carmen, giving Annie a smile.

"Yeah," said Lauren. "I'm lost without my derby wife."

"You didn't look lost to me," Annie said. "You were wicked out there."

Liz looked across the rink at where the High Rollers were stretching. "I can't help feeling like it's their fault that you got hurt," she grumbled.

Annie shook her head. "I was the one who let anger get the better of me."

"But that Dee Stroyer egged you on," said Holly bitterly. "She went for the jugular."

Annie couldn't help but look surprised that this remark had come from Holly.

Holly rolled her eyes. "I know, I know, I'm one of the biggest 'eggers' in the league. But when I do it, it's only jokingly."

"She's right," said Sharmila. "If Dee hadn't taunted you, you wouldn't have reacted the way you did, Annie."

"Mentioning Tyler was hitting below the belt," Carmen agreed.

Annie was genuinely touched by how protective her team was being on her behalf. They were right. Dee had wanted to infuriate Annie with all those cracks about asking Tyler to the dance. So maybe Annie and Dee were equally to blame for Annie's injury. "Well," she said, "it's over and done with, and there's really nothing we can do about it now."

As the High Rollers went into a huddle and sang one of their psyche-out chants, Holly flashed a mischievous grin. "Not necessarily."

"Uh oh." Liz frowned, planting her hands on her hips. "What are you suggesting, Holly Terror?"

Holly shrugged. "Just a little play-acting. All in good fun, of course, but I say we make the Rollers think we're a bunch of crazed maniacs! I bet then that Dee Stroyer, and everyone else for that matter, will think twice about pushing our buttons."

Sharmila's vivid green eyes twinkled. "Sounds like fun."

"Sounds like a stint in the sin bin," Liz corrected.

Holly shook her head. "Not if we go *wild* before the scrimmage."

Lauren cocked her head. "Huh?"

"Watch and learn, freshman," said Holly. By way of demonstration, she gave the unsuspecting Sharmila a good hard shove.

Caught off guard, Sharmila went spinning across the track, just barely managing to stay on her feet.

"That'll teach you to mess with my skates!" Holly barked.

Sharmila didn't miss a beat. "Touch me again, Red, and I'll mess with more than just your skates."

Annie's eyes were wide as Holly skated out until she was standing toe stop to toe stop with Sharmila.

"Oh yeah?"

"Yeah!

By now, Jesse had joined Annie on the sidelines, curious about the screaming match.

"What's going on?" he asked.

"They're putting on an act," said Annie, watching as her two teammates began to circle each other like panthers ready to attack.

Holly was positively screeching now. "Listen up, Godzilla..."

"You put your grubby little paws on me again and I will take you out!"

"Please!" Holly rolled her eyes. "The only thing more fake than your threats is—"

"Your hair colour?" Sharmila shot back.

That did it! The Belles and the Rollers watched in stunned silence as Holly flung herself at Sharmila, grabbing her by the shoulders. But Sharmila was ready. She wrapped her arms around Holly's waist and squeezed.

"It's a brawl!" cried one of the Rollers.

"Look at them go!" said another.

Liz allowed the girls to pretend a little longer before she grabbed Lauren and they skated out to break up the fight. Liz hauled a hissing and sputtering Holly off Sharmila, while Lauren secured Sharmila's arms behind her back.

"Guess you didn't hear what I said about people keeping their hands to themselves!" Sharmila screamed. In the next second, she'd ducked out of Lauren's hold and was pulling Holly across the track by her ponytail.

Carmen giggled. "My turn," she whispered to Annie, then bombed out to the track to throw herself on Liz.

"Do something!" cried Annie, grabbing Jesse's arm. "Somebody's gonna get hurt."

"Nah," said Jesse, grinning. "They'll be fine. Nobody's even gonna break a nail."

Annie glanced at the High Rollers who were watching the fight in amazement. A few of them looked a little nervous, and Annie didn't blame them.

Then came the peal of a whistle and Coach Ritter barrelled across the track, stopping on her toes in the centre of the action.

"Enough!" she shouted.

The girls immediately ceased their faux-kicking and mock hair-pulling, and caught their breath.

Annie watched as the High Rollers exchanged glances. She was pretty sure that for the most part they knew the whole brawl had been a sham, but a few of them looked worried that the Belles had anger management issues.

At that moment, Coach was looking pretty angry herself.

"What in the world was *that?*" she demanded.

"Theatrics," said Holly. "We just wanted to remind them who they're dealing with, that's all."

"Who they're dealing with," said Coach sternly, "is a well-trained team of athletes who should know better than to behave like a bunch of psychos on the track!"

"We just wanted to scare them," Liz said sheepishly. "We

wanted them to think we were loose cannons, so they'd be less likely to mess with us."

Coach sighed. "I understand," she said. "I do. You're upset because their antics are partially to blame for Annie's injury. But in my opinion, nonsense like that is what gives roller derby a bad name. If we want this sport to be taken seriously, we have to behave like serious athletes – at all times."

Holly lowered her eyes. "It's my fault, Coach," she confessed in a mumble. "The whole thing was my idea."

Annie was pretty certain Coach would have surmised that without a confession.

Coach was quiet for a long moment. Then she sighed heavily. "OK. You don't intimidate an opponent by out-bragging, out-threatening, or out-trashing them. You do it by going out there and out-skating them. Never again, team. Do I make myself clear?"

The girls nodded, and murmured, "Yes, Coach." Even Annie, who hadn't actually taken part but felt guilty by association, muttered an apology.

She decided to take Coach's advice to heart. Next time Dee Stroyer or anyone else got under her skin, she would just have to rise above it and make it about the skating and the skills.

Not about Tyler Erickson.

Coach gave a firm nod. "Now," she said, "get yourselves together. The scrimmage starts in five."

A few of the girls went to the lockers to splash cool water on their sweaty faces. Sharmila stayed behind to deal with her long, gorgeous mane of velvety black hair. The melee had caused it to come loose from the French plait she wore. When she accidentally dropped her hairband, Jesse practically dived to pick it up from the floor.

Or at least that's how it seemed to Annie.

"Nice work out there," Jesse said, handing Sharmila the band. "You got out of Lauren's half nelson without batting an eyelash. You were like Houdini or something."

Sharmila laughed. For a second, Annie couldn't believe that this feminine giggle was coming out of the same tough brawler she'd just seen on the track.

Annie fiddled with the stopwatch as Jesse continued to talk to Sharmila, who expertly folded her long glossy hair over and over itself until the plait was back in place.

Annie wasn't sure why Jesse paying attention to a pretty girl should bother her. Maybe she was just feeling jealous because she was certain that Tyler would never look at *her* that way now – not after she humiliated him by turning him down for the dance.

She didn't get to think about it much longer, because her teammates were returning from the locker room and the High Rollers were already on the track preparing to scrimmage.

"Thanks for the show," Dee Stroyer said in a sarcastic voice. "Maybe next time you can do *Wicked* for us." Then she let out a nasty, sarcastic laugh.

Annie gritted her teeth and vowed that next time, she'd put Dee Stroyer in her place.

The only problem was she'd have to get back on her skates to do it.

Chapter Twelve

The next evening, Annie went to Coach Ritter's house to babysit Abbey and Brandon. Coach had a meeting with her boss at the hospital and promised she would only be gone a couple of hours.

"Brandon will tell you he doesn't have to eat his broccoli, but that's a lie," Coach explained, slipping a lightweight scarf around her neck. "And Abbey will probably play the 'five more minutes' game when bedtime rolls around." She smiled at Annie, whispering as she buttoned her coat. "Here's a trick. Start getting her ready for bed fifteen minutes early, then you can give her three five-minute grace periods. You still get her to bed on time, but she thinks she's getting away with something."

"Brilliant," giggled Annie.

"Survival instinct," teased Coach. "You've got to stay one

step ahead of them at all times."

"Just like roller derby," Annie observed.

"Yes, except around here, I don't have a referee."

Coach left for her meeting and Annie locked the door behind her. She found Abbey and Brandon waiting for her in the kitchen. Abbey had nearly cleared her plate, but Brandon, as predicted, still had a pile of broccoli on his.

"I don't wike bwoccli," he said, folding his arms firmly across his chest.

It took some cajoling on Annie's part and one exceedingly animated telling of *The Three Little Pigs* to get him to gobble down the remaining vegetables.

Later, while the kids enjoyed their dessert in front of the television, Annie loaded the dinner dishes into the dishwasher and put away the milk carton. As she did, she couldn't help engaging in a cheesy fantasy about being married to Tyler and having two adorable kids.

She was startled out of her daydream when she closed the fridge door and found Abbey smiling up at her; the little girl was holding a battered scrapbook.

"What's that?" Annie asked.

"You'll see!" cried Abbey. Then she bounded off into the living room.

Annie followed her and found both kids beaming at her from the sofa. Between them, the album was open to a photo of a stunning young woman on roller skates.

"Oh my God!" cried Annie, taking in the permed hairstyle

and high-waisted acid-washed jeans. "Is that your mummy?"

Abbey nodded, pointing to the photo. "She was a roller derby girl in college."

Annie laughed, sitting down and taking the scrapbook into her lap. "This is great," she said, flipping the pages. There were several more pictures, even a few action shots which showed how aggressive Coach Ritter had been on the track. There were also several newspaper clippings which attested to the fact that "Miss Demeanor" had been a star.

They giggled over the photos for a little while, then Annie had to break the terrible news that it was time for bed.

"I can get ready myself," Abbey informed Annie with a big smile. "But can I have five more minutes?"

Annie laughed. "Sure."

Brandon protested, but only mildly. He was so sleepy he could barely keep his eyes open. Annie got him into his pyjamas while Abigail headed to the bathroom to brush her teeth.

"Sleep tight, poppet," Annie whispered, tucking Brandon under the puffy blue quilt.

"Wait. Where's Quackers?"

"Crackers?" Annie was confused. "You just had cookies."

"No." Brandon shook his head. "Quackers is my duck." He let out a huge yawn.

Annie searched around the room for a plush toy duck, but Quackers wasn't under the bed, in the toy box, or in any of the dresser drawers.

"Try the hamper," Abbey suggested, appearing in the

doorway wearing a pink ruffled nightgown. Backwards. Annie opened the dirty clothes hamper. In addition to a pair of blue jeans with grass stains on the knees and a little sweatshirt streaked with finger paint, she also found Quackers!

"Thank you," said Annie, grinning at the little girl. "You just earned yourself five more minutes!"

Abbey clapped her hands.

"Here you go," she said, tucking the well-loved, worn-out yellow duck in beside Brandon.

"Ask him if he used the potty," Abbey instructed.

"Did you use the potty?" Annie asked.

"I don't hafta go," said Brandon, closing his eyes.

Annie turned off the light and tiptoed out of the room. Then she helped Abbey adjust her nightgown and they spent the next fifteen minutes curled up on her pretty quilt, where all Abbey could talk about how one day she would be a roller girl.

"Just like your mum!" said Annie.

"And just like you!" said Abbey.

When Abbey finally nodded off, Annie went downstairs to begin her homework. She got her maths out of the way first, then read a few chapters of *Wuthering Heights*. Three minutes into an essay on the First Continental Congress her phone chirped.

"Hey, Lex," she said, accepting the call.

"How's the child wrangling going?" Lexie joked.

"They're cute," sighed Annie. "But exhausting."

They talked about school for a bit, and Annie floated the idea that maybe she should approach Tyler and ask him out. "I'm just

133

afraid I've blown any chance I ever had with him," she grumbled.

"It's his loss," Lexie said. "He's a moron if he can't understand why you didn't want to let down your team. Try to put him out of your mind."

"He's too cute not to think about!"

Lexie giggled. "True. But you know who else is cute?"

"Who?"

"Duh. Jesse! He's also cooler and nicer than Tyler."

"He's also in love with Sharmila."

"*What?!* Since when?"

"I don't know," said Annie with a deep sigh. "Maybe since forever. You should have seen the way he looked at her the other day at the rink."

"Sounds like you're jumping to conclusions," said Lexie. "If you ask me, if he likes anyone, it's—"

Lexie's observation was cut off by the sound of a scream from the upstairs hallway. "Gotta go!" cried Annie, hitting the phone's off button. She leaped out of her chair and ran.

At the top of the stairs she heard Brandon's voice crying, "Quackers! Quackers, you got flushed!"

These words were followed by uncontrollable sobbing coming from the bathroom.

Unfortunately, that wasn't the only thing coming from the bathroom.

Annie looked down to see that a steady flow of water was already seeping into the hall carpet.

She dashed into the bathroom, where Brandon was wailing.

The feet of his pyjamas were soaked through, and a steady cascade of water continued to bubble up and out of the toilet. Annie began grabbing anything she could to mop up the flood – tissues, bath sheets, even a plush chenille bathrobe she found hanging on a hook behind the door.

But the waterfall did not stop.

Annie gave up; she splashed across the tile floor, picked Brandon up and sat him on the edge of the sink. As the toes of his pyjama feet dripped into the deluge, she took out her phone and called home.

"Dad ... ? *Help!*"

Eventually, they were able to piece together the events that had led to the fact that Annie's father was now standing above the Ritters' toilet with a plunger.

Brandon had got up to use the bathroom, but in his groggy state, he'd accidentally dropped poor little Quackers into the toilet, then flushed before he realized his toy had decided to go for a swim.

The good news was that Quackers had been rescued and was soaking in some strong detergent in the bathroom sink.

The bad news was that the toilet was currently out of order until Coach Ritter could bring in a plumber.

Annie was helping Brandon into a dry pair of pyjamas when the front door opened.

"Hello?" came Coach's anxious voice up the stairs. "Annie? I saw your father's car in the driveway and…"

"We're up here," called Annie.

She could hear Coach taking the stairs two at a time. When she flew into Brandon's room, her eyes were filled with panic. "Is everything all right? Is anyone hurt?"

"Just Quackers," said Abbey, who was perched on the foot of her brother's bed.

"He awmost dwowned!" Brandon reported, then, to clarify, he added, "in the toywet."

Coach's eyes went from Brandon, to Abbey, to Annie, and finally to Annie's dad, who had just appeared in the doorway, holding the plunger. It only took her a second to figure out the specifics, and when she did, to Annie's surprise, Coach burst out laughing.

"Didn't I tell you?" she asked. "I really do need a referee."

It took some persuading to get the kids back to sleep after all the excitement. Coach had to reassure Brandon several times that Quackers would dry out and recover. In the meantime, Abbey offered him her favourite stuffed dinosaur to sleep with, which Annie thought was the sweetest thing ever.

Finally, both children conked out and Annie and Coach Ritter tiptoed down the stairs.

Dad was waiting in the living room, flipping through

the scrapbook.

"Well, that's embarrassing," laughed Coach when she saw what he was looking at. "Those were my big hair days! Have you ever seen anything so unflattering?"

"Don't be silly," said Dad. "I've always found the frizzy perm a very becoming look." He managed to say this with an utterly straight face, but Annie noticed that his eyes were twinkling with laughter.

Coach rolled her eyes and smiled. "You're either a true gentleman, or you really need to have your eyes checked."

Annie wasn't sure she liked the flirty tone in either her father's or Coach Ritter's voice. It was just too … weird.

"I'm really sorry about the mess, Coach," Annie piped up, eager to change the subject.

"Oh, honey, it's not your fault at all. In fact, this isn't even the first time something like this has happened to ol' Quackers. Let's see … there was that one time he went through the dishwasher, and then the time he nearly got devoured by the neighbour's labradoodle." She shook her head, chuckling. "Believe me, that little duck has had more than his share of near-death experiences. But he always bounces back."

Annie sighed. "I hope the same can be said for the toilet."

"Fished a toy car out of there just last week. We've got the plumber on retainer."

"Well," Dad said, laughing, "I'm very impressed with how calmly you're taking this."

"It's part of the job description," said Coach. "Now, David, may I offer you a cup of coffee for your trouble?"

Annie watched as a strange expression flickered across Dad's face. He looked as though he really wanted to accept the offer, but after a moment's hesitation he shook his head.

"Thanks, but I've got an early start tomorrow, and I'm sure Annie's still got homework to finish."

For some reason, Annie was relieved to hear him decline.

"Maybe another time?" he added.

"I'd like that," said Coach. She gave Dad a glowing smile, which he returned with a bashful grin.

Annie just stood there, feeling like a spare part. Suddenly, she was in a hurry to go home.

"So," she said, as soon as Dad began backing out of the driveway, "do you like her?"

She'd considered being more subtle, but then decided to be direct. She wanted an answer, so she might as well just come out and ask the question.

"Of course I like her," said Dad. "She's your coach."

"Not what I meant," said Annie. "I was asking if you *like* her. Meaning, do you want to date her?"

Dad frowned. "Would that be a problem?"

Truthfully, Annie wasn't even sure. Part of her loved the idea of Dad having someone to spend time with. Coach Ritter was fun, smart, and pretty. Dad could do a lot worse.

But there was another part of her that still hoped for a miracle. There was always that slight chance that Dad and Mum would get back together, and she was afraid that Dad dating would be a step away from that possibility. "I don't know," she answered finally. "I honestly don't know. All I do know is that I want you to be happy."

Dad smiled. "Back atcha, Beanie," he said softly.

Annie closed her eyes and they drove the rest of the way home in silence.

Chapter Thirteen

As Halloween approached, the buzz around school about the dance increased. Pretty much everyone who intended to go had asked or been asked and the couples were obsessing about their costumes. From what Annie had heard in the halls and cafeteria, there were going to be an awful lot of Bella and Edwards bopping around the dance floor. There would also be a few Raggedy Ann and Andys, and a handful of Superman and Wonder Woman pairs.

Before their first class, Annie and Lauren hung up posters all over school. Lexie had made the original drawing and Annie thought it was brilliant. It was a sketch of two roller girls, one dressed as a witch and the other as a vampire, facing off on the jammer line. She'd made the wheels on their skates neon so they'd catch people's eyes.

Annie had just pinned one up on the bulletin board outside the art classroom when two junior girls came sauntering down the hall. They stopped at the board and studied the poster.

Annie and Lauren pretended to be engrossed in a flyer advertising SAT tutoring, so they could eavesdrop.

"Roller derby?" said one. "Are they kidding? Who would waste time watching a bunch of sluts on wheels beat each other up?"

Sluts on wheels? Annie felt the insult like a kick to the solar plexus. Did people really think that?

"Don't they know it's on the same night as the dance?" said her friend. "What kind of loser would choose roller derby over the coolest dance of the year?"

When the junior girls flounced off, Annie turned to Lauren. "Sluts on wheels?" she asked, aghast. "Is that really what they call us?"

"I guess so," said Lauren. She looked equal parts angry and heartbroken.

"That's ridiculous." Annie shook her head. "They think we're slutty just because we wear fishnets?"

"Who knows?" Lauren shrugged. "Maybe they just don't get that roller derby is a real sport!"

"If they'd come to the bout they'd know," Annie said, sighing. "But I'm starting to feel like we're putting this exhibition on for nothing."

Which means I turned down Tyler for nothing. Annie felt miserable.

It was one thing to sacrifice a date with Tyler Erickson to take part in a bout that was going to attract lots of fans, but to miss the Halloween dance when no one was even going to show up...

And, what's more, she might not even be able to skate!

Tessa came around the corner just as the class bell rang. Even though Annie was now completely crutch-free, they'd got in the habit of walking to English together.

"Hi, Tessa," said Lauren.

"Hey." Tessa turned to frown at the poster. "I hate to tell you this but you know the poster you hung up outside the chem lab?"

Annie nodded. "What about it?"

"Somebody took a magic marker to it."

"Oh, no!"

"Let me guess," sighed Lauren. "Someone drew moustaches on the faces?"

"Among other things," said Tessa with a grimace. "To put it delicately, the roller girls are now anatomically correct."

Annie gasped. "They didn't?!"

"They did!"

"That's just rude," said Lauren. "Did you take it down?"

"I was going to," Tessa replied, "but the principal beat me to it."

Well, that was a relief. Annie could only imagine how furious Lexie was going to be when she heard that someone had defiled her drawing.

Lauren excused herself to rush off to her History class and Annie and Tessa headed to English. Along the way they stopped to put up a poster outside the music room, and another on the bulletin board near the main office.

Tessa chatted pleasantly about how excited she was that she and her whole team, the Derby Dolls, would be coming to watch the Halloween bout, and how the Liberty Belles were going to look so awesome dressed as vampires. Annie laughed and agreed, but no matter how much she nodded and smiled, she just couldn't stop the phrase "sluts on wheels" from ringing in her ears.

They got to English before the bell.

Annie almost wished they'd been late. Because what she saw when she walked into the classroom made her sick to her stomach.

Tyler, looking gorgeous as always, was seated at his desk.

And Kelsey was draped across the top of it.

OK, maybe "draped" was a little dramatic. But she was posing with her perfect legs crossed and her shoulders back, tossing her hair like she was caught in a hurricane. Kelsey seemed to be completely engrossed in whatever it was Tyler was saying, and every so often she'd let out a giggle.

So that's what flirting looks like, Annie thought glumly, sliding into her desk behind Tyler's.

When the bell rang, Kelsey slipped gracefully off the desk and put her hand on Tyler's shoulder. "I can't *wait* for Saturday night," she said.

Annie's heart sank as she realized that Tyler must have asked Kelsey to the dance. Annie felt her throat tighten and there was a stinging sensation behind her eyes. But there was absolutely no way that she would allow herself to cry! Not here. Not now. It was highly likely that later, at home, she'd curl up in a ball on Granny's ugly tartan sofa and sob her heart out. But she wasn't going to let Kelsey have the satisfaction of seeing that she'd won.

As Annie forced her eyes to remain dry, she tried to work out why Tyler had even pretended to be interested in her in the first place. Obviously he hadn't really liked her all that much if he could so easily bounce back from her rejection to ask Kelsey out.

As Ms Schwarz began her discussion of the doomed love between Heathcliff and Catherine, Annie tuned out. Any other day she would have been fascinated by the study of such an iconic literary masterpiece, but today she simply didn't give a hoot about the fictional characters' heartache.

Today, she had her own broken heart to deal with.

Annie was sitting on the sofa, half-heartedly doing her ankle exercises when the doorbell rang.

The bad mood that had begun before English class in response to the sluts on wheels remark (and had steadily declined when she'd witnessed Kelsey flirting with Tyler) was only getting gloomier now as she worried about her chances of skating on Saturday. The rehab exercises didn't hurt like they had at the beginning, so that had to be a good sign. And she was walking perfectly now, without even a hint of a limp.

But walking and skating were two very different things, and

she knew it would all depend on what Dr Borden said at her appointment tomorrow. The suspense of not knowing was really taking its toll.

The bell rang again; Annie got up and went to answer the door.

"Who is it?" she called out.

"Reverse trick-or-treater!" came a friendly voice.

"Huh?" Annie laughed as she swung open the door to see Lauren grinning on the front porch. "What on earth is a reverse trick-or-treater?"

"Someone who doesn't wear a costume and brings *you* candy!" Lauren explained, producing an enormous bag of miniature chocolate bars from behind her back. "Ta da!"

There was a snuffling sound from below and Annie looked down to find the saddest and sweetest looking creature she'd ever seen.

"Who's this?" she cooed, crouching down to scratch the animal's long droopy ears.

"This is Prudence," said Lauren, giggling as the basset hound gave Annie a big, sloppy kiss on the cheek. "She's slobbery, but lovable."

"Well, come in," said Annie. "Both of you."

Lauren gave a gentle tug on Prudence's lead and the squat canine waddled into the house.

"I'm so glad you came over," said Annie, as she and Lauren flopped onto the living room sofa. "I was feeling kind of low, actually. It's nice to have a visitor." She glanced down at Prudence, and corrected herself. "Visitors, that is."

Lauren opened the plastic bag and offered it to Annie who helped herself to a handful.

"You have no idea how much I need this," she said, sighing. "I had a horrible day."

Lauren peeled back the wrapper on a mini Snickers and nibbled on the end. "The posters, huh?"

"That was the beginning of it. But then it got worse. I think Tyler is taking Kelsey to the Halloween dance."

Lauren paused mid-nibble. "Oh, Annie. I'm so sorry."

"So am I," Annie admitted. "I really thought he liked me. I mean, I turned him down for the dance but that didn't mean…" She trailed off with a shake of her head. "I guess in a perfect world he would have understood. I mean, he would have been disappointed, but he would have asked me to do something the following weekend, and then…"

Lauren gave her an understanding smile. "And then you'd live happily ever after, right?"

"Something like that."

"Well, in case you haven't noticed," said Lauren. "This isn't a perfect world. And if one exists I'm pretty sure it's in a whole other galaxy." She motioned to the television, where an extremely slender girl in a very tight dress was trying to convince them that her brand of long-wearing lipstick was the only one worth using. "For example, if this were a perfect world, that supermodel would weigh more than a child, and I wouldn't have had to sneak this Halloween candy out of the house in order to keep my mother from flipping out."

Annie felt bad for her friend. "You're in terrific shape. You're one of the most powerful skaters on the Belles and you've got great stamina and muscle tone."

"Thanks." Lauren bit into another chocolate bar. "It's weird, ya know? Part of me is actually fine with the way I look. And then sometimes there's a part of me that wishes I could go into your closet and borrow a pair of skinnies or a one of your pencil skirts." She shrugged. "I swear, if I dropped ten pounds my mother would be so deliriously happy, she'd probably spring for a whole new wardrobe."

Annie considered this for a minute. Then she took the big bag, fished out four more fun-size bars, and closed the bag. "How about we set a limit," she said reasonably. "Two more each, and save the rest for Halloween?"

Lauren smiled. "I can live with that."

Annie doled out the chocolate – a Snickers and a Milky Way for her, a Kit Kat and a mini bag of peanut M&M's for Lauren.

Annie couldn't help but wonder, if her parents hadn't split up and her mother had come to America with them, would her and Lauren's mums have been friends? She thought about how her mum was so against her playing roller derby, how she would have preferred her to take up something "sensible" (and less dangerous), like tennis, or golf. Annie couldn't imagine anything more boring than hitting a ball around a court.

Annie was willing to concede that Lauren's mother had every right to be concerned about her daughter's health, but she suspected Mrs DeMarco was more motivated by the idea of Lauren wearing nice clothes than she was about cholesterol levels.

She sighed. *Why can't mothers just accept their daughters the way they are?* she wondered.

As the advert for lipstick gave way to one featuring models strutting across the screen wearing push-up bras and very little else, Annie remembered the junior girl's unkind comment about roller girls.

"Do you think most people agree with what that girl in school said about us?" she asked. "You know … that roller girls are really just…"

"Tramps on skates?" Lauren finished for her.

"Well, her exact words were 'sluts on wheels'," Annie pointed out. "But it means the same thing."

Lauren reached down to scratch Prudence on the head. "I guess maybe they assume we are because our outfits can be a little on the sexy side."

"Oh, please," said Annie, rolling her eyes. "Have you seen the cheerleading uniforms? The short little skirts and those midriff tops? Those are much more revealing than our outfits. And I've seen girls come to school dressed way sexier than we do on the track. That doesn't make them sluts."

"People just say things," said Lauren. "Even when they don't know what they're talking about."

"I know!" Annie shook her head. "I mean, the last thing anybody could call me is a slut. I've never even been—" She stopped short.

Lauren gave her a sideways grin. "Never even been what?"Annie felt her face turn pink. "Never mind. You'll laugh."

"No I won't." Lauren raised her right hand and put the other on top of her Kit Kat bar. "I swear on my chocolate I won't laugh!"

"OK." Annie smiled. "I was just going to say that you can't really call someone a slut if they've never even been ... kissed."

Lauren's eyes flew open. "You've never been kissed?"

Annie shook her head.

"But you're so pretty. And cool. I would have guessed you had tons of boyfriends back in London."

"You would have guessed wrong, then," said Annie, laughing. "I mean, I had a few crushes over the years, but I never actually had a boyfriend. I spent a lot of my time doing gymnastics, so I missed out on most of the parties my classmates started throwing in secondary school."

"What about dances?" Lauren asked.

"I went to one school disco at the end of Year Eight," said Annie, giggling as the memory came back to her. "Only one boy asked me to dance. His name was Bernard and he was the shortest boy in our year. Unfortunately, I had just begun my infamous growth spurt, so his nose was even with my..." She motioned to her chest.

Lauren cracked up. "What a nightmare!"

"Tell me about it!" Annie opened her Milky Way and popped the whole bar into her mouth. "How about you?" she asked.

"Ever played tonsil hockey with a boy?"

Lauren looked at her like she was crazy. "Tonsil hockey?"

"I heard it in a movie once. That's not what it's called here?"

"Most people call it hooking up, or making out."

"OK, then," said Annie. "Have you ever hooked up with a boy?"

Lauren didn't answer but her cheeks went completely red, which of course was an answer in itself.

Annie let out a gleeful little shriek. "You *have!*"

"OK, I have. But believe me, it wasn't what you're imagining. No violins playing in my head. To be honest with you…" Lauren cleared her throat and shrugged. "Kissing boys really isn't all that. It didn't do much for me at all."

"Well, that was probably because you were beginners, and your technique lacked polish," said Annie. "C'mon! I need details."

Lauren sighed. "It was on vacation last summer. I met a boy on the beach. I was just looking for a friend to hang out with, but apparently, he had other plans. On the last night of our stay the resort hosted a clambake with a bonfire, and while we were sitting around the fire…" She shrugged again. "He kissed me."

"That's so romantic!"

"Not really." Lauren laughed. "He'd eaten two lobsters, a ton of clams, and about a zillion pounds of coleslaw. Five minutes after we kissed, he ran under the pier and puked his guts out."

"No!"

"Yep."

"Oh, Lauren!"

"I felt so bad for him! We decided that we were going to just stick to being friends, and we still talk on Facebook every now and then, but as you might imagine, we steer clear of the topic of seafood."

Annie laughed so hard she thought she might wet herself. When she was finally able to catch her breath, she reached over and gave Lauren a hug.

"Thanks, Lauren. I really needed some cheering up today."

"Glad I could be of service," said Lauren, snapping the Kit Kat in half and taking a bite. "And who knows, maybe it'll even help your ankle."

"How's that?"

"Haven't you ever heard the saying 'laughter is the best medicine'?"

"Well, in that case…" said Annie, reaching for the TV remote.

They watched the comedy channel for the rest of the afternoon.

Chapter Fourteen

Annie sat on the exam table, tapping her foot.

She and Dad had just come from the radiology department where she'd had another MRI scan, then Martha had set them up in one of the examination rooms to wait for the doctor.

Tap. Tap. Tap.

The scan would show whether she could skate on Saturday...

Tap. Tap. Tap. Tap.

...or she couldn't.

TAP-TAP-TAP-TAP-TAP-TAP-TAP-TAP-TAP-TAP-TAP—

"Annie!" Dad reached over and planted his hand on Annie's knee. "Stop that! You're tapping so hard you're going to sprain your ankle all over again."

Annie forced her foot to keep still, but her insides continued to churn. It meant so much to her to take part in the Halloween bout. The whole thing had been her idea! Missing it was simply unimaginable.

Finally, the door opened and Annie sprung off the table, landing solidly on both feet without so much as a twinge. But it wasn't Dr Borden. It was a petite woman with iron-grey hair and a pair of wire-rimmed glasses perched on her nose.

"Nice dismount," joked the doctor. "Hi, I'm Dr Delaney."

"It should be," chuckled Dad, "considering how much money we spent on private lessons and training time."

"How's my ankle?" Annie blurted out. "Can I skate tomorrow night?"

Dr Delaney slipped the MRI scan into the light box on the wall. Annie's foot appeared in negative exposure.

"Such a lovely likeness," teased Dad. "I think I'll have it framed and hang it over the mantle."

Annie knew he was trying to keep the mood light, in case Dr Delaney was about to deliver bad news. But she couldn't take the suspense even one more minute. "Is it better?"

Dr Delaney pointed to the scan and smiled. "You're all better!"

"Seriously?"

"Good as new!"

Annie threw her arms around her dad, then around the doctor. "Thank you!" she cried. This means I can skate tomorrow night!"Dr Delaney's smile flickered slightly. "Well, technically, yes."

Dad went instantly on alert. "Technically?"

Dr Delaney removed her glasses and looked at Annie. "Dr Borden told me you suffered this injury while playing roller derby, is that right?" Annie nodded.

"Well, from a medical standpoint, there's no reason you shouldn't be able to skate on it. But from a purely practical point of view, I have to say, I question the wisdom of continuing to take part."

Annie blinked. Dr Delaney questioned the "wisdom" of roller derby? What?

"Maybe I'm just old-fashioned," said Dr Delaney, raising an eyebrow at Dad. "And of course this is just my personal opinion, but don't you think roller derby is a bit high-risk?"

Dad threw Annie a warning glance before he answered. "I did, at first," he admitted. "But this injury was an anomaly. Annie's actually a very good skater."

"I see." The doctor pressed her lips together. "Well, as I say, it's just my opinion." She turned to Annie. "If you feel any pain, I would advise stopping immediately and icing it, but I think you'll be fine as long as you wear an ankle brace."

"Thank you," Annie said again. But this time she skipped the hug.

In the car, Annie felt like she might explode.

"The nerve of her!" she huffed, buckling her seat belt. "Would she have said something like that to a *boy*? Would she have told a *boy* that hockey or football was too high-risk?"

"She may have," Dad allowed.

"And what about girl figure skaters? They don't even wear pads or helmets, and everybody thinks they're just darling. I'm sure jumping in the air and spinning four times is pretty high-risk. But just because they wear sparkly dresses, nobody has a problem with it."

"I think you're generalizing," said Dad. "And the doctor wasn't saying anything you haven't already heard. There's no denying that derby – like football and figure skating – can be dangerous."

"Dr Borden told me he's going to let his kids try derby when they're older," Annie reminded her father. "So clearly he doesn't see anything wrong with it."

"Calm down," said Dad, patting her hand. "I'm just saying you should at least try to see it from the doctor's perspective." He paused. "And Mum's. You know she only has your best interests at heart, don't you, Beanie?"

So that's what this was about. Annie immediately felt guilty. "You talked to Mum?"

"Well, somebody had to. Apparently, you haven't answered any of her calls for the last few days."

"I'm sorry about that, Dad. I just knew that if we spoke, we'd fight. And I wasn't in the mood." She gave him a nervous look. "What did she say?"

"That she still wants you to find another interest."

Great. "And what did you say?"

"I told her that while we respected her feelings about roller derby, you and I both felt that it was a perfectly safe sport if you wear the proper equipment. I said there was no reason why you should quit." He beamed at Annie. "How awesome am I, huh?"

Annie laughed. "Pretty awesome!" she said. Then she looked at the dashboard clock.

"Dad ... do you think if we hurry we can stop at home, grab my gear, and make it to the rink in time for me to catch the last half of practice?"

"Sorry, Beanie. It'll take too long to go all the way home; we'll never make it in time."

Annie frowned.

"Which is why I packed up all your stuff before we left the house and put it in the car!"

He jerked his thumb towards the back seat, where Annie's derby duffle bag sat.

Seeing it almost brought tears to her eyes. "Did I say 'pretty awesome'? Sorry, I meant the most awesome dad in the whole world."

"That sounds like me," said Dad. "And now ... to the rink!"

"To the rink!" Annie echoed. "And step on it!"

The Liberty Belles broke into cheers when Annie appeared on the sidelines in full gear, plus, of course, her new ankle brace.

"You can skate?" Lauren asked.

Holly rolled her eyes. "No, she can't. She only put her T-shirt and wheels on to mess with our heads."

"I can skate," Annie confirmed, giggling.

Coach Ritter appeared and gave Annie a huge hug. "OK, here's how it's gonna be, kiddo. You stretch out completely – no shortcuts. Once you're warm and limber, do some nice easy laps. Take it slow. Don't be a hero."

"Gotcha," said Annie.

While her teammates went back to the drill they'd been working on when she'd arrived, Annie dutifully did her stretches. It felt good to be moving again, even if her muscles protested a bit. She finished limbering up just as the Belles were leaving the track for a water break. Perfect timing … Annie would be able to do her laps without getting in anyone's way.

She glided out onto the track, surprised by how giddy she felt. Taking a deep breath, she pushed off and began to roll.

It felt wonderful! It was like being reunited with an old friend. The breeze in her face, the rumbling vibration of the wheels, the stinging in her quads as her legs worked harder and harder.

She had to concentrate to keep herself from taking off at top speed. But Coach was right. She'd need to ease into it if she didn't want to damage her ankle.

"Looking good out there, Turner," called Sharmila.

"You'll be ready to kick butt tomorrow night!" Carmen assured her.

Annie did one more lap and joined her teammates, who'd

finished their break and were ready to resume practice.

"Annie," said Coach Ritter. "How about you pick the next drill?"

"Really?" Annie beamed. "OK ... um ... how about we go for Bus Driver?"

A few of the girls groaned, because this drill could be a really painful test of quad strength, but most of them welcomed the opportunity to work their all-important thigh muscles.

"You got it, kid!" laughed the coach. "And you can be the driver!"

The Belles took their places at the four different "bus stops" around the track. Since the driver was meant to be seated as she drove the imaginary bus, Annie lowered herself into a deep squat and began to skate. She stopped to "pick up" the "riders", and soon she was driving the entire team around the track, setting the pace, stopping and going at her own whim.

"Tunnel!" she shouted.

Obediently, the girls dropped to an even lower squat.

There were shouts for mercy, and quite a few muttered curses. Annie felt a fine film of perspiration on her forehead and her quadriceps burned. But she knew she'd be grateful for the strength and stamina she was building.

"Look out for the debris in the road," Liz called from the back of the bus, and the girls all pretended to jump over something in the middle of the track.

Someone grunted. Then someone else said, "I hate the bus – I'd rather take the train!" Those who weren't gritting their teeth in agony actually laughed.

Finally, Coach Ritter blew her whistle to end the drill.

"Excellent work, Belles! I have to say, I've never coached a bunch of girls with such a great work ethic!"

"Think we can beat the High Rollers tomorrow night?" Liz asked.

"You betcha," said Coach. "And even if you don't, I want you to have fun. The exhibition should be a celebration of teamwork and friendship. It should be an opportunity to show people how great derby can be!"

As the girls dispersed, Annie sat down on a bench and began to unlace her skates. Her thighs were burning as though she had molten lava instead of blood coursing through her veins. It hurt, but she loved it. It meant she'd worked hard. It meant she was back!

Jesse appeared and sat down beside her, handing her a bottle of juice from the snack bar. "So is that the same old ankle you used to have?" he asked. "Because based on the way you were skating just now it looked like maybe they secretly replaced it with a bionic one."

Annie laughed. "If that's your way of saying I haven't completely lost my touch, then thank you."

"You looked great out there, considering you haven't practised in two weeks. Guess that means you're a natural."

"Thank you again." Annie blushed at his flattery. "You know what's completely weird?"

"Um…" Jesse frowned in thought. "Lexie's taste in clothing?"

Annie giggled. "No. What's weird is that two months ago I had never even heard of roller derby. But now I feel like I really can't live without it. Well, OK, I *could* live without it, but I definitely wouldn't want to."

"Wow," said Jesse, smiling. "You've got it bad."

"I do!" cried Annie. "I really do. These last two weeks have been horrible. Without derby – the skating, the competition, the people – I actually felt…" She bit her lip, searching for the right word. "Incomplete."

She expected Jesse to laugh at her dramatic description, but to her surprise he didn't. "I get that," he said. "I totally get that. When you find something you really connect with, that's exactly how it is. It feels like…"

Annie met his deep blue eyes. "Feels like what?" she asked.

"Like falling in love," said Jesse softly. "That's what you sounded like just now. Like you've fallen in love."

His words seemed to go straight to her heart. For a moment, her whole body felt a little fluttery, but that was just silly. This was Jesse, not Tyler. She and Jesse were just friends. And they were talking about roller derby, not falling in love with a person.

Maybe she was just a little light-headed from so much skating. Whatever it was, it was gone as quickly as it had come.

"I guess I did sound like that," she said, blinking to break the spell of his storm-coloured eyes. "I'm just so glad to be back."

"It shows," said Jesse, chuckling as he got up from the bench. "I've gotta go download some more Halloween tunes for tomorrow night. Any suggestions?"

"How about 'Monster Mash'?"

Jesse laughed. "Gimme a little credit, huh? That's a classic. It's the first one I bought."

"OK, OK, don't get cocky." Annie rolled her eyes and thought. "'Scary Monsters', by David Bowie," she offered.

Jesse grinned. "Already got it."

"Hmm." Annie thought for another second. Then her eyes lit up. "Oh!" she cried, certain she'd come up with one he hadn't thought of. "Alice Cooper's 'Feed My Frankenstein'?"

Jesse's eyes danced. "Got that one, too."

He began to walk away, but after a few steps he turned to smile at her over his shoulder. "Guess you and I are on the same wavelength, Anne R Key," he said. And then he winked!

Chapter Fifteen

Boo.

That was the first syllable that came into Annie's mind when she awoke, smiling, on Saturday morning.

Her first American Halloween.

She tossed off her duvet and hopped out of bed, dressing quickly in jogging bottoms and a hoodie, then she laced up her trainers and hurried downstairs.

There was a lovely late-autumn chill in the air and she breathed deeply as she began her jog up the driveway. Her plan was to take a nice easy run to Rosie Lee's and admire the Halloween decorations along the way.

Her neighbourhood had certainly gone all out.

She loved the rustic look of tall yellow-brown corn stalks

tied to pillars and lamp posts, and the pumpkin and hay-bale arrangements on porches. She got a particular kick out of the whimsical witch-crashed-into-a-tree that decorated the big old oak in Lexie's front garden. And, of course, any house where kids lived had smiling pumpkin lanterns on the steps.

It would be even better at night, she knew. Annie couldn't wait.

Her leg muscles were tingling and her breath was coming out in frosty little clouds as she approached Rosie Lee's. It was only eight on a Saturday morning, but she was pleased to see that there was a little crowd in the shop.

There was a table of women by the window enjoying tea and scones as they held their regular book club meeting. A young husband and wife with a baby in a stroller looked sleep-deprived, but happy to be having a quiet moment in the sunny little café. He was sipping coffee; she was trying not to nod off in the middle of her lemon-poppy seed muffin. Annie hoped they'd notice her babysitting flyer on their way out. They looked like they could really do with her services.

Annie wasn't surprised to see the sweet, elderly couple she'd invited in the day she'd been handing out flyers. They had become regulars and waved to her when she entered.

"No witch costume today?" the old man teased.

Dad was hustling around behind the counter. He looked up from a cappuccino he was frothing and smiled. "Hey there, String Bean!"

"Good morning!" Annie unzipped her hoodie. "I came to

help you box up the confetti cupcakes for Mrs Brentwood," she explained, making her way towards the kitchen. "Two dozen, right?"

"Three," Dad corrected. "She called last night and ordered another twelve."

"Wow, that's gonna be some party."

"Right?" Dad put the steaming cappuccino on a little tray, and headed towards the book club ladies. "She invited us, by the way, but I told her we'd be at the bout. Oh, hey, do me a favour, Beanie. Turn on the radio, will you? I've been so busy I haven't had a chance."

Annie hit the button for the café's "sound system", which was really just a fancy CD player with an AM/FM radio.

As she went into the kitchen to begin boxing up the cupcakes, the DJ's voice gave way to the silly lyrics of "Monster Mash".

Annie smiled because the song reminded her of Jesse. The invigorating run, the spooky decorations, and the pleasant scene in Dad's café had all combined to put her in a great mood. And tonight promised to be even better – she would finally be skating in a bout after more than three weeks off! And of course there was the post-bout Halloween party Liz's parents were hosting for the Belles.

Annie sighed happily as she began arranging the gorgeously iced cupcakes in a white cardboard box. Halloween was going to be amazing.

If she could just manage to keep her mind off Tyler holding Kelsey in his arms, it might just be perfect!

* * *

Johnny Rotten smiled a snaggle-toothed grin at her from his place on her front steps.

Not *the* Johnny Rotten, the legendary punk rocker from the 1970s; Johnny Rotten the pumpkin lantern, who was making a special Halloween appearance on the Turner's front porch – courtesy of Lexie and a really sharp knife!

"It's uncanny," Annie giggled, wiping the slimy pumpkin innards off her hands. "It looks just like him."

"Thanks," said Lexie, who'd been the one to carefully draw the singer's likeness on the orange plant before allowing Annie to carve it out. "And the funny thing is that in about two weeks, he'll really live up to his name." She thumped the firm fresh pumpkin shell and smiled. "This jack-o'-lantern will be so rotten he'll have maggots."

"Lovely thought," said Annie, wrinkling her nose.

It was six o'clock and the sky was a lovely shade of cobalt behind the silhouetted branches of the nearly leafless trees. The air was crisp and all along Annie's street, porch lights were being turned on.

"It's show time!" cried Lexie, lighting a stubby little candle and placing it inside Mr Rotten's empty head. "Let's get our costumes on for the trick-or-treaters."

That was fine with Annie. She couldn't wait to get into her vampire outfit!

Upstairs, she dusted her face with white powder to create a

creepy pallor, then she lined her eyes with black kohl and used a deep purple eyeshadow to give her eyes a sunken look. She outlined her lips heavily with black and filled them in with dark red lipstick, drawing a red "dribble" out of the corner of her mouth. It looked like she'd just made a fresh kill and there was blood trickling down her chin. False eyelashes would be her only concession to glamour tonight. After all, her persona was a "sexy" vampire.

She bent over at the waist and shook out her hair. With Lexie's help, she teased it within an inch of its life and coated it with nearly an entire can of maximum hold hairspray.

When she flipped to an upright position she looked in the mirror and gasped.

"I like it," said Lexie, nodding. "You've got this kind of elegant undead look. Very enticing."

Annie didn't disagree. Although she couldn't imagine how much conditioner she was going to need tomorrow to detangle her undead hairdo.

As Lexie went into the bathroom to put on her costume, Annie slipped into the vampire dress her friend had designed. As per Dad's instructions, they'd shortened the slit that ran up the leg and added a little more fabric to the neckline. But even with these alterations, the dress still showed off Annie's long legs.

All that remained was to pop the plastic fangs into her mouth. Just as she was doing that, Lexie burst out of the bathroom and flung her arms open wide.

"*Estoy aquí!*" she announced in Spanish. "Translation:

here I am!"

Annie's fangs literally dropped out of her mouth. "Ohh-kaay," she said. "*Here* you are … but I have absolutely no idea *what* you are!"

"You mean *who* I am?"

"Fine," Annie giggled, taking in the man's suit and tie and the thin black stuck-on moustache that curved up wildly at each end. "Who are you?"

Lexie twirled one end of the curly moustache and said, "Only the greatest surrealist painter who ever lived." She took a debonair bow. "The artistic genius, Salvador Dali!"

"Lexie, that's incredible. You look just like him … well, almost."

Annie had seen paintings by Dali in the museums back in London. In her opinion, the only word to describe both the artist and his work would be "bizarre".

"I'm going to go out on a limb here and guess that you'll be the only person in Liberty Heights dressed like that." She readjusted her plastic teeth and laughed. "Maybe even the whole world."

"That, of course, was my intention," said Lexie. "Now, let's go introduce some trick-or-treaters to surrealism."

"I think they'd rather we introduce them to chocolate," said Annie.

Lexie rolled her eyes. "And that, *mi amiga*, is the problem with America's youth!"

Laughing, the girls headed downstairs.

* * *

After a steady stream of princesses, ballerinas, devils, clowns, and superheroes, Annie was getting anxious. She knew it was still ages before she had to be at the rink, but she just couldn't wait any longer.

"Let's just leave out a bowl of treats," she suggested, closing the door on a giggling bunch of witches and monsters. "We can leave a note that says 'help yourself' and go to the rink right now. We can start putting up the decorations."

"It's way too early," said Lexie, peering out of the front window. "Coach Ritter isn't even there yet."

"How do you know that?"

"Because she's standing on your front porch."

On cue, the doorbell rang, and Annie tugged open the door with a big, fang-filled grin.

"Trick or treat!" sang Abbey and Brandon.

"Oh my goodness," cried Annie in mock alarm. "What have we here?"

"I'm a roller girl!" announced Abbey, showing off her skates and elbow pads.

"And I'm a fwireman!" Brandon pointed to his red helmet.

"Well, please do come in," said Annie, happy to see that Abbey wasn't afraid of her costume this time. Even Coach had dressed up – she was wearing a sequined cowboy hat, a chequered shirt, and cowboy boots.

"Giddy-up," she quipped, following the kids into the hallway.

"Coach, you look terrific," said Annie.

"I couldn't agree more," came a voice from the kitchen doorway.

Annie glanced back to see Dad standing there, smiling. He was holding rather than wearing his werewolf mask, which was a good thing given Abbey's aversion to it.

"Howdy," said Coach, tipping her hat to him.

Annie noted the batter-and-icing-smeared apron Dad was wearing over the furry suit and torn clothing that made up his werewolf costume. "Were you baking?" she asked.

Dad nodded. "I'm going to bring some goodies to sell at the bout," he explained. "Sort of a fundraiser for the team. I just thought of it this morning and when I called Sus— I mean, Coach Ritter, she thought it was a great idea."

This was news to Annie. She managed to stop herself from blurting out, "You *called* her?" but she was pretty sure her surprise was written all over her face.

After a couple of minutes of chat, Coach Ritter said it was time to be going. They had a few more visits to make before heading to the rink.

"I'll see you later," said Dad, then added quickly, "at the bout, of course." Then he ducked back into the kitchen to finish the cupcakes.

"See you in a bit," said Coach.

Brandon and Abbey thanked Annie and they were off.

While Lexie stepped into the bathroom to adjust her moustache, Annie lingered in the open front door, watching

Coach and her little ones go. Dad and Coach Ritter … talking on the phone! Did it mean anything? And if it did, how did she feel about it?

She didn't get to mull it over for long; just as Coach and the kids disappeared around the corner, two more trick-or-treaters started up the Turner's front path.

Annie had to laugh at this unusual pair. The little one, who Annie guessed was around seven, had long brown hair covered with a wide red bandana wrapped around her forehead. She also wore a fake tattoo sleeve and a Guns N' Roses T-shirt.

"Wow!" cried Annie, smiling at the little girl as she climbed the porch steps. "It's Axl Rose, right here on my front doorstep!"

"You were right, Jesse!" little Axl cried, turning to her big brother, who was sporting a black top hat, black afro wig, and press-on nose ring. "She knew exactly who we were!"

Annie smiled at the Slash impersonator standing at her door. "Great costumes," she said.

"I had a feeling you'd appreciate them more than the soccer moms on the block."

Annie dug into the bowl and dropped an extra hefty helping of treats into Axl's plastic pumpkin. "You'll need energy if you're planning on trashing any hotel rooms later," she said. "I'm Annie, by the way."

"I'm Katie. I'm only Axl Rose for tonight."

"Did I hear someone say Axl Rose?" called Dad, once again appearing from the kitchen. He took one look at Jesse and Katie, smiled broadly, and began to sing "Welcome to the Jungle" at the top of his lungs.

"Well now I know where Annie gets her awesome taste in music," said Jesse.

Lexie, returning from the bathroom, shot Jesse and his sister a grin.

"Nice to meet you, Axl. I'm a really big fan of yours." To prove it, Dad launched into a few bars of "Patience" as he made his way back to the kitchen.

"OK, rock star," said Jesse, adjusting Katie's bandana. "We can hit about three more houses before it's time to get you home."

Katie gave Annie a big smile. "Thanks for the candy, and good luck in the bout tonight, Anne R. Key!"

This took Annie by surprise. "You know my derby name?"

"Sure," said Katie with a shrug. "I know you came from England and you used to be a gymnast. Jesse talks about you all the—"

"All right then!" Jesse said quickly. "Gotta be going now. See you at the rink."

As he hastily turned to leave, Lexie cried out, "Wait!"

Jesse turned back.

"Before you go, one question…" She did a slow turn, showing off her costume. "Who am I?"

"That's easy," said Jesse. "Salvador Dali."

"That proves it," said Lexie, as she and Annie watched Jesse and Katie hurry down the path.

"Proves what?" asked Annie.

"He's the perfect guy."

Annie gave Lexie a genuinely bewildered look. "For who?"

"*Seriously?*" Lexie stared at her for a long moment, then rolled her eyes and sighed. "Let's go to the rink," she said.

But Annie was already out of the door.

Chapter Sixteen

In Annie's opinion, not since the Twilight saga had a bunch of vampires looked so good.

Carmen was a 1970s vampire, wearing dangling disco-ball earrings and a smiley face T-shirt with the words "Have a Nice Day" printed on it. Sharmila was a vampire nerd complete with taped horn-rimmed glasses, bow tie, argyle socks, and a "Kick Me" sign stuck to her back. Liz had borrowed Coach Ritter's cowgirl hat and was wearing a pair of rhinestone-encrusted holsters on a leather belt slung low around her hips. Lauren was surprisingly believable as a vampire biker chick, in a leather jacket and Harley-Davidson T-shirt.

And Holly ... well, she outdid everyone! She was dressed in jet black from head to toe; she had fangs, like Annie, but in addition to these, she wore a headband with two pointy ears on it.

"I don't get it," said Lauren. "What kind of vampire are you?"

In reply, Holly grinned and raised her arms to reveal two enormous black wings. "I'm a vampire *bat*!"

"Brilliant!" said Annie, laughing along with the others.

While the Belles touched up their spooky make-up, the High Rollers arrived in the locker room. They were already in their witch costumes, and although their outfits lacked the creativity of the Belles', Annie had to admit they looked pretty spooky. They all wore heavy green face paint and a few of them had glued on fake warts.

Their captain, Allison, was the only exception; she was dressed as a good witch in a shiny silver dress and a white conical hat with pink feather trim. Her eyes were enhanced with extra-long blue glitter false lashes.

True to form, Holly kicked off the trash talking.

"Hope you girls are ready to work some magic, because you're gonna need to cast a major spell to beat us tonight!"

"Please!" huffed Allison, waving her glow-stick wand at Holly. "We'll be sending you vampires home in your coffins!"

"Did you say 'vampires'?" said Dee Stroyer, sending a wicked look in Annie's direction. "I think you mean 'tramp-ires'!"

Annie immediately jerked her plunging neckline up a little.

"Don't listen to her," Carmen whispered. "You look amazing. She's jealous, that's all."

Annie smiled gratefully, but she couldn't help feeling self-conscious.

"That was uncalled for, Dee," said Allison, frowning at her teammate.

Dee made a face and rolled her eyes.

"C'mon, Annie," said Lauren, taking her arm. "Coach wants us to sell tickets."

Annie was more than happy to get out of the locker room. The more distance between her and Dee Stroyer, the better.

All the posters the girls had put up around town and at school had really paid off! To Annie's surprise the turnout was amazing. People of all ages were streaming into the rink, and what was even better was the fact that most of them were in costume.

As she and Lauren handed out tickets and counted change, Annie felt positively elated. "This is great," she said. "I never dreamed so many people would show up."

"Hey, there's your doctor," said Lauren, pointing towards the middle of the queue.

Sure enough, Dr Borden, his young twins, and a pretty woman Annie assumed was his wife were waiting to purchase their tickets. Martha and her husband were with them.

"I guess that's one way to drum up business," joked Annie. "Sprain something!"

Lauren laughed.

The next customer was completely unrecognizable in a hideous monster mask that made Dad's werewolf head look like a cuddly puppy.

"How many?" Annie asked hesitantly.

"One," the monster grunted, handing Annie the money.

Annie handed one ticket to the monster.

"Thanks, Annie," he said but his voice was so muffled inside the mask she couldn't place it.

Annie watched him shuffle away and continued to watch until he disappeared into the crowd. *Must be someone who knows me from school*, Annie thought.

She was jolted out of her thoughts by the sound of her phone ringing. She answered it without even checking the number.

"Hello?"

"Annie, love. It's Mum!"

The sound of her mother's voice after so long made Annie's heart swell. She hurried to a quiet corner where she wouldn't be overheard.

"Oh, Mum," she began, her words coming out in a flurry of emotion. "I was so rude the last time we talked, and I've been avoiding your calls. I'm so sorry!"

Back in London, Mum laughed and Annie could hear the relief in it. "I know, darling. I know. Dad explained how upset you were and I realized I was being unreasonable. So I'm sorry, too."

Annie smiled. "Mum, you should see me right now. I'm wearing a vampire costume my friend Lexie designed!"

"Sounds incredible! Get Dad to take a photo so you can send it to me."

"OK."

"Well … I just wanted to wish you good luck in your match tonight."

Annie stopped her from pointing out that it was actually called a bout. Mum was making a huge effort and that was all that really mattered. "Thanks. Maybe someday you'll be able to see me skate. I think you'd be really proud of me."

"I'm always proud of you, honey," said Mum, and Annie could hear the catch in her voice. "Always."

Annie felt tears forming in her eyes. Despite the complicated nature of their relationship, she really did love her mother. She wiped her eyes, careful not to smudge her make-up. "I miss you, Mum," she said. "I'll call later and let you know how it went."

She hung up and went back to the ticket table, only to find Lauren closing up shop.

"Time to skate," she said, grinning at Annie. "Ya ready?"

Annie smiled and pulled her helmet on over her teased hair. "You have no idea!" she said.

Laughing, they headed for the track.

"Ladies and Gentleman!" came Jesse's voice through the loudspeaker. "Please welcome the Liberty Belles … although tonight, they're going by a different name!"

On cue, AC/DC's rock anthem "Hells Bells" exploded through the rink and the crowd roared.

Annie swore she could feel the music pulsing inside her as she and the team skated in a pace line, then as a wall, shouting, waving and blowing exaggerated kisses to the unprecedented crowd. After two exhilarating laps, they skated to the sidelines to make way for their opponents.

"And here come the High Rollers!"

Jesse segued out of "Hells Bells" into the lyrics of The Doors' "Roadhouse Blues". Jim Morrison wailed, "Let it roll, baby, roll…" and again the fans went wild.

While their opponents worked the crowd, Liz had the Belles huddle up for a quick pep talk. "I want you all to remember that tonight is about having fun!" she said. "I know the Rollers aren't exactly the most sportsmanlike team in the league, but like Coach said, let's not sink to their level. There are lots of people watching tonight and we want to show them what derby is really about!" She turned to flash a big grin at Annie. "OK, Annie, how about you start us off as jammer?"

Annie felt a rush of excitement as she got into position.

Unfortunately, standing right beside her on the jammer line was Dee Stroyer.

"Might wanna take it easy tonight, tramp-ire! Don't want to hurt that ankle again, do you?" Annie opened her mouth, hoping a snappy retort would come to her. But of course, no such luck.

In fact, suddenly the only thing she *could* think of was how incredibly badly her ankle had hurt when she'd fallen on it three weeks before.

Annie knew a threat when she heard one!

Chapter Seventeen

The ref blew his whistle and the bout began.

Annie's head swam as she ran on her toe stops and zoomed around the track. She was the jammer – she had a job to do!

She let her body do the work, pushing and gliding…

But Dee's cocky remark about hurting her ankle kept whirling in her mind. Annie winced, remembering the sharp pain and the lingering ache.

The three weeks without skating!

If she fell again, what would happen? Was her ankle more vulnerable now? She had her ankle brace on, but was that enough?

Dee had her head down, skating hard.

Annie was right beside her, matching her stroke for stroke.

She could pass Dee with just the slightest effort.

But what if…?

Maybe it wasn't even a conscious decision, but in the next heartbeat, Annie felt herself tightening up … holding back … and slowing down.

Dee took lead jammer position. Annie stayed close. But not close enough.

Four points later Dee slapped her hips to call off the jam. The crowd cheered and the Rollers celebrated with high fives and gleeful shouts.

Annie had accomplished nothing!

She hung her head, skating towards the side.

Liz was next to her immediately. "Shake it off, Annie! It's only the first jam. We'll get 'em!"

Annie nodded. She bent down, resting her elbows on her knees to catch her breath. *Shake it off,* she repeated in her mind. *Don't let Dee Stroyer psyche you out.*

She stood up and carefully rotated her ankle, then flexed it.

No pain. She was fine. *Stop being such a wimp.*

"You OK, kiddo?"

Annie looked up from her skates to see Coach Ritter.

"I'm fine," she said. "Honestly fine."

Coach frowned. "Even so, let's not press our luck with that ankle. Take a breather."

As Annie took her place on the bench, she glanced into the crowd. Lexie and Tessa, who were sitting with her teammates, were waving, but they both looked a little concerned – worrying about her ankle, obviously. She let her gaze sweep the spectators again. And there he was.

Madly pumping his fist in the air and shouting like crazy, it was the hideous masked monster who'd called her by name at the ticket table.

When he saw that Annie had spotted him he waved.

Without even thinking, Annie waved back. Then she smiled and the monster threw both hands into the air in a gesture of triumph.

Annie couldn't help but laugh at his enthusiastic support. But she was thoroughly puzzled. *Who are you?* she wondered. *Take off the mask!*

When Annie joined the pack for the third jam, Jesse blasted Talking Heads' "Psycho Killer" and Annie decided with a snarky grin that she'd dedicate this song especially to Dee Stroyer. As David Byrne sang, "Better run run run run run run run away…" she imagined herself belting them out, right in Dee Stroyer's face! She felt her confidence return in a powerful rush. *Thanks, Jesse. I owe you one!*

The whistle blew and the roller girls took off.

Holly was amazing! Fast and skilful, she bombed around the track with a take-no-prisoners smile on her face. When the jam finished, Holly had scored seven points and lifted her arms in triumph to show off her bat wings. Jesse responded by blasting a snippet of Meatloaf's classic "Bat Out of Hell" and the crowd went absolutely crazy!

When one of the High Rollers, Mae Hem, was given a penalty

against Lauren for an illegal elbow block, the ref appealed to the crowd with a knowing smile. "How about we spin the penalty wheel?" he cried.

The crowd cheered their approval.

Annie laughed; she hadn't even realized that the High Rollers had set up one of these wheels before the bout. It was basically a large, circular piece of cardboard that whirled on a spinner, a big version of what you'd get in a board game. The High Rollers had divided the spinner into six triangular sections. Each section depicted a silly activity, such as a "Tug of War" or the "Hokey Pokey", to be performed by the player who'd been given the penalty and the opponent she'd fouled.

Laughing and hooting, the players from both teams skated to the sidelines, leaving Mae Hem alone on the track, pretending to be furious with her punishment. The "Penalty Mistress", who was dressed like a circus ringmaster (and whom Annie recognized as Slammy Tammy), spun the wheel.

It landed on "Pillow Fight".

Again, the crowd roared with delight.

Mae Hem scowled and shook her head as Lauren was led back onto the track by the referee. Each girl was given a long stocking cap and a matching granny-style nightgown to pull on over her derby uniform, then they were handed oversized bed pillows.

The whistle blew, and Jesse immediately played Metallica's "Enter Sandman".

The crowd went crazy as Mae and Lauren began to pummel

each other with the pillows.

When the whistle blew again, the ref asked the fans to decide by applause who'd won the fight. The decision went to Lauren, which meant the High Rollers had to give up one of the points they'd already scored.

Mae's fury went from fake to authentic as she made her way to the sin bin to endure her penalty. Then the bout resumed.

Just before half-time Liz scored thanks to some hard-core blocking by Sharmila. Then Sharmila and Allison the good witch performed an impromptu routine in which Sharmila the vampire nerd removed the Kick Me sign from her own back and sped around the track after Allison, finally catching her and sticking the sign on the back of her silver dress. All the other Rollers then surrounded their captain and pretended to land kicks on her backside. The crowd laughed and cheered as the girls retreated to the side of the track to take their mid-bout break.

"That's what I call a half-time show," said Lauren, skating up beside Annie.

"I know, isn't it great?" she beamed, looking around at the crowd. She was surprised to see that quite a few kids from high school had actually shown up. What was even better was the fact that they really seemed to be enjoying themselves.

But then she remembered that right now Kelsey was probably snuggled up against Tyler, dancing to some pop ballad and whispering sweet nothings in his ear.

So much for triumph.

Shake it off, she told herself for the second time that night.

Then Coach Ritter came over and quickly checked Annie's ankle. "Looks OK, but if you want to rest it for a jam or two, I'll understand."

Annie shook her head. "No thanks. It feels great and I'm not even tired. I'd really love to be jammer again, Coach."

"We'll see," said Coach.

Half-time ended and the girls took to the track. When Annie heard a series of wolf whistles, she turned to scan the crowd, certain it would be Dad, pretending to be a werewolf. But then she remembered he was the timekeeper, and at that moment he happened to be consulting with a sideline ref. So it couldn't have been him whistling.

Lexie? Annie wondered, but realized immediately that if Lexie were capable of whistling like that, Annie would have heard her do it before. And Jesse was too busy tinkering with the sound system to whistle at her.

Curious, she continued to search the faces – some masked, others made-up – seeking out the whistler. And then the sound came again, followed by a shout, "Hey, Anne R. Key! Give 'em hell, baby!"

Annie's eyes swept the crowd in search of where the deep, masculine voice had come from.

The masked monster!

"Looks like you've got a fan!" said Lauren, giggling. "Who is it?"

"I have no idea!" breathed Annie.

"Too bad he looks like Frankenstein's uglier brother," Lauren teased, pointing to the rubber mask.

"Well," joked Annie, laughing as the masked monster pressed a hand to his distorted rubber lips and blew her a kiss, "looks aren't everything."

In the first few minutes the Belles scored three more points. Pleased with their lead, Coach waved Annie over.

"Ready to be jammer again, kiddo?"

"Absolutely!"

"Well, then," said Coach, laughing, "like the guy in the rubber head said, give 'em hell!"

That was exactly what Annie intended to do.

As the jam kicked off, Jesse played "Werewolves of London" and Annie felt a surge of power because she knew the song was a tribute to her.

Once again, she found herself facing off against Dee.

As they took their places on the line, Dee opened her mouth, ready with a rude remark. But to Dee's shock, Annie narrowed her eyes and spoke first.

"I've had it with your mouth, so why don't you save us both the trouble and keep it shut for a change?"

Dee gaped at her, speechless.

The whistle blew and the teams took off, skating hard. The rowdy fans sang along to "Werewolves of London" and in Annie's mind they were all singing just for her, especially when they howled along with Warren Zevon as he wailed out the "Ahhhh-OOOOOHHHH" refrain again and again.

In no time, she became lead jammer. And on her second lap of the track Annie passed through the pack again, scoring four points.

In the crowd, Dad and Lexie went nuts, and the masked monster shouted her name!

But the attention Annie was getting seemed to rile Dee. Furious, she slammed into Annie from behind.

The ref's whistle blared. "Penalty!"

Fuming, Dee rolled towards the sin bin, flashing a fiery look in Annie's direction as she went.

Annie actually laughed. She wasn't scared any more. If anything, she was exhilarated. With Dee out of action for a full minute, Annie would have the opportunity for a power jam.

As play resumed, the Belles skated as though they were of one mind. They formed a wall, expertly blocking in one of the Rollers' blockers, which forced the rest of their blockers to stay near. This left Annie with a free lane, and she took full advantage of it. She flew around the track, letting the fans' cheers fuel her as she racked up an impressive thirty-seven points!

The bout ended in a dazzling victory for the Liberty Belles and the team collided in a joyous group hug. In the centre of the happy huddle, Lauren caught Annie in a crushing grip, which Annie returned.

"We're tied for first place in the league!" cried Lauren.

"I know!" Annie shouted back. "I don't think anything on earth could be better!"

But as it turned out, Annie was dead wrong about that.

Because when she looked into the crowd she saw the masked monster removing the ugly rubber face.

And underneath it was Tyler.

Chapter Eighteen

Annie could only stare.

As she followed her team off the track to the sidelines, she was vaguely aware of the High Rollers joining the Belles to shake hands and offer their good-natured congratulations.

Then Jesse was there, holding up a high five, which she accepted, but she still couldn't bring herself to take her eyes off Tyler.

"That power jam was unbelievable!" said Jesse. "You totally owned it!"

"Uh huh," said Annie, her gaze still locked on Tyler. "I mean … thanks."

"Listen," said Jesse, leaning closer so only she could hear him. "I know it's kind of lame, but I was wondering if you might wanna—"

He stopped talking when he realized that Annie was still staring straight ahead. He followed her gaze, and frowned deeply when he saw who she was looking at.

"Great," he grumbled. "So *he's* a derby fan now?" Annie felt a little flutter in her chest and smiled. "Looks like it."

Jesse shook his head. "I'll see ya later, Annie," he said, then turned and walked away.

But Annie was still too focused on Tyler to even notice.

His blond hair was rumpled from having spent so much time beneath the monster head, but it only made him look more boyishly handsome. He was smiling at her and Annie could have sworn those green eyes were actually sparkling.

Now he started walking towards her. She wished she could take at least one step in his direction, but she remained rooted to the spot, heart pounding like a drum. Then again, maybe he'd think she was playing hard to get by allowing him to come to her. She'd heard some guys liked the thrill of the chase. She sincerely hoped Tyler Erickson was one of them.

When Tyler reached her, he said, "You were amazing out there, Annie!"

"Thanks," she managed to say. "But, um, what are you doing here?"

"Watching an extremely cool sport I didn't even know existed," he said, chuckling. "Although, I gotta say, if someone had told me there was a sport where the girls wore fishnet stockings and dresses like that, I probably would have checked it out a lot sooner."

Annie felt her cheeks flush as she realized he was referring to her sexy vampire dress. *God bless you, Lexie Jones! I owe you big time!*

"Seriously though," Tyler was saying, "I was totally impressed."

"I'm glad you enjoyed the bout," said Annie, relaxing enough to give him a smile. "But I thought … I mean, I was under the impression you were going to the dance." *With Kelsey*, she added silently.

"Well, I was planning to go," he said in a teasing voice, "but see, the girl I really wanted to take had other plans. Something about a roller derby bout."

Annie's breath caught in her chest. So he *hadn't* asked Kelsey after all. Annie had turned him down and he hadn't asked anyone else! It was all she could do to keep from bursting into a dance of absolute joy! "Oh," she managed to say.

"Ya know," he said, reaching out to brush a strand of teased hair off her forehead, "the dance will be going on for at least another two hours. As long as we're already in costume…"

Annie swallowed hard, holding her breath…

"…do you want to go with me?"

Don't scream. Don't throw yourself into his arms. Just say yes.

"Yes."

"Great. Why don't you go change out of those skates and I'll meet you out front?"

"Perfect," said Annie, giving him what she hoped was an alluring smile.

She watched him make his way through the crowd and out of the door.

"Hey!" cried Lexie, bounding up to her and giving her a hug. "What exactly did I just witness between you and Tyler?"

"He asked me to the dance! He still wants me to go with him!"

To Annie's confusion, Lexie didn't begin jumping up and down and shrieking with delight. "Oh."

"Oh? Is that all you can say?"

Lexie shrugged. "Well, I mean, I'm happy for you. But what about the party at Liz's house? The whole team's going, and Liz said that since I'm the official costume designer, I'm invited, too."

Annie felt her stomach drop to her skates. In the excitement of Tyler asking her to the dance – *again* – she'd forgotten all about the party Liz's folks were hosting for the Belles. She glanced over her shoulder to where her teammates continued to celebrate their win. Some of them were making plans to car pool over to Liz's house. Others were chomping into what was left of Dad's collection of baked goods.

"I don't think they'll mind if I miss the party," she told Lexie. "Do you?"

Lexie's reply was a disapproving silence.

"They know how much I like Tyler. They were so sweet the day I had to turn him down. Some of them even told me I should miss the bout to go out with him, because it would be my first American high school dance."

"That was very understanding of them," said Lexie quietly. "And loyal."

Annie sighed. "It's just one party. Honestly, I'm sure they'll be OK with it."Before Lexie could say any more, Annie felt two hairy arms encircle her from behind. "Way to go, Beanie!" her father cried. "You were outstanding!"

"Thanks, Dad."

"Why don't you go grab your things and I'll drive you to the party?"

Annie wriggled out of Dad's hug and bit her lower lip. "About the party ... I was thinking I might skip it. I've just been asked to the dance at school."

Dad seemed a little surprised, but he was also clearly pleased. "That's exciting," he said cheerfully. "I'm sure it will be a lot of fun."

Annie gave Lexie a look that said, "See?"

Lexie just rolled her eyes and walked away.

Annie turned back to her father with a hopeful look. "So I can go to the dance?"

"Sure," he said. "Just tell Jesse I'd like him to have you home by midnight."

Annie blinked, confused. "Jesse?"

"Isn't that who asked you to the dance?"

"No, of course not!" Annie laughed. "In fact, I doubt Jesse Matthieu would ever be caught dead at a school dance! And besides, he doesn't think of me like that."

Dad looked as though he wasn't entirely convinced, but thankfully, he didn't say so. "Well then, who's the lucky guy?"

"Only the coolest, cutest, most popular boy in the whole

school. Tyler Erickson."

"Ah," said Dad, nodding. "The soccer star."

"Yep!" Annie was smiling so broadly she thought her cheeks might pop. "It's still OK if I go, isn't it?"

"It's still OK."

Annie clapped her hands. "OK, great! I'll see you at midnight, not one minute later, I promise!"

"Have a good time, Beanie. But Annie…"

"I'll be on time, Dad," Annie said, laughing. "After all, I don't want to turn into a pumpkin."

Annie was about to sprint off to the locker room when Coach Ritter appeared at Dad's side, smiling. "Ready to go, David?"

David? What happened to Mr Turner?

"You two are going somewhere?" Annie asked, forcing her voice to remain casual.

"Susan and I are just going out to celebrate the win with a cup of coffee," said Dad. "And it's also a good chance for me to check out the local coffee shop competition."

Annie was surprised to realize that the idea of Dad and Coach chatting over a cup of coffee – some place where Dad wouldn't have to be the one to brew it – actually made her happy. "Well then, you have fun, too." She gave her coach a big grin. "Just have him home by midnight!"

"Will do," said Coach. "And, Annie, I'm so proud of you! You really proved yourself to be a true roller girl tonight!"

Annie thanked her, but deep down inside, she felt the slightest pang of guilt.

Would a true roller girl miss a team victory party to go to a dance with a boy?

Maybe. If the boy was Tyler Erickson.

Annie pushed away the guilty feeling and hurried to the locker room to change out of her skates. Minutes later, she was rushing through the rink, dodging the lingering fans who were picking up schedules for future bouts.

As she reached the door, she caught sight of Jesse. He was helping his little sister put on her jacket.

"Hey, Jesse…" Annie called.

She thought she saw him lift his head at the sound of her voice, but instead of turning in her direction, he continued to zip up Katie's jacket.

Guess he didn't hear me, Annie thought. She briefly considered going over to say goodbye, but then she spotted Tyler through the glass doors. He waved and smiled.

The flutter turned into a full on shiver as she pushed open the door and went out to meet him on the pavement.

"Ready, roller girl?" he asked in that flirty voice.

"Ready," Annie said, returning his smile. "I hope you're not disappointed that you weren't able to go to the dance as David Beckham."

"Well," said Tyler. "I'm sure you would have made a gorgeous Posh Spice, but this is fine too."

As they started walking, Tyler took her hand.

As far as she was concerned, this was miles better than fine.

Annie's first American Halloween was officially perfect!

ALL ABOUT Roller Derby

RULES OF THE GAME

A roller derby game is called a bout. A bout usually lasts sixty minutes and is divided into two-minute jams. During a jam, each of the two teams have five players on the track, all skating in the same direction. The blockers and pivots form a tight pack. The two jammers start behind them and race to break through the pack. The first jammer through the pack is designated the lead jammer. However, no points can be scored until the jammer passes the pack for a second time. The jammer then scores a point for every opponent that she overtakes, provided she passes the player in bounds and without penalties. Both jammers may score points for the duration of the two-minute jam or until the lead jammer calls off the jam. A jammer typically scores four points every time she makes it through the pack. If she overtakes the other jammer she scores a fifth point, and this is known as a Grand Slam. The team with the most points at the end of the bout wins.

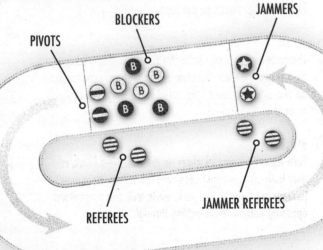

BLOCKERS

JAMMERS

PIVOTS

REFEREES

JAMMER REFEREES

SKATER POSITIONS

⭐ **JAMMER**

The jammer wears a helmet cover with a star and is the only player who can score points. To score points, a jammer must break through the pack once and sprint around the track. A jammer scores a point for every opponent she passes on her subsequent passes through the pack.

LEAD JAMMER

The lead jammer is the first jammer to break through the pack and pass all the opposing blockers and pivot. The lead jammer may choose, at a strategic time, to call off the jam to prevent the opposing jammer from scoring. She does this by putting her hands on her hips.

⊖ **PIVOT**

The pivot acts as a pacesetter for the team and is designated by a striped helmet. The pivot calls out plays and provides guidance for the rest of the team. The pivot typically stays in front of the blockers.

Ⓑ **BLOCKER**

Each team has three blockers on the track. The blockers play both offensive and defensive roles. They help their jammer get through the pack, while trying to prevent the opposing jammer from getting through.

PENALTIES

There are many rules in the sport of roller derby, enforced by referees and non-skating officials (NSOs). If a skater commits a major penalty, she is sent to the penalty box, also known as the sin bin, for sixty seconds. If a jammer is sent to the penalty box, the opposing team's jammer scores a point for the missing player if she passes through the pack. If both jammers are sent to the penalty box, the first jammer is released as soon as the second jammer reaches the box.

OFFENCES RESULTING IN A MAJOR PENALTY INCLUDE:

- ☒ Tripping an opposing player
- ☒ Back blocking
- ☒ Using elbows to the chest or face
- ☒ Swearing at another skater or referee
- ☒ Blocking twenty feet ahead or behind the pack
- ☒ Deliberately falling in front of another player
- ☒ Grabbing, pulling or pushing an opposing player

HISTORY OF ROLLER DERBY

Roller derby was first played in the 1930s and quickly evolved into a popular spectator sport, thanks to staged crashes and collisions. By 1940 it was watched by about five million spectators, but by the 1970s the sport had faded into obscurity. At the beginning of the twenty-first century, a roller derby revival began in Austin, Texas and soon spread to many other cities and countries. Modern roller derby has focused on athleticism rather than showmanship. It is the fastest-growing sport in America, and is under consideration to become an Olympic sport at the 2020 games!

Read on for a sneak peek at the next
Roller Girls book...

In a Jam

"Goooooooal!" the announcer shouted. "The Liberty Heights Stags now lead the Prospect Park Panthers 3-2 in the final game of the season!"

Annie squealed and hugged her best friend standing next to her. "Did you see that, Lex? My boyfriend scored a brilliant goal!"

My boyfriend. Just the sound of those words made her tingle with excitement. Tyler was by far the fittest guy at Liberty Heights High School. He had irresistible blond hair that always seemed to fall just right and green eyes that Annie could gaze into for hours. And his body… wow! Lean and muscular, he was perfect. And he was all Annie's. She couldn't believe her luck.

Lexie grunted and looked up briefly from her sketchbook.

"He's awesome. Can we go now?"

"'Course not," Annie said. The cheerleaders came out and did a little number led by Annie's least favourite person in the world. Blond, popular, and with a personality to match the Wicked Witch of the West, Kelsey had been vicious to Annie since she moved there. They'd got off to a bad start just because Annie had accidentally knocked into Kelsey on her Rollerblades. Their relationship had got even worse when Annie turned down a spot on the cheerleading squad to play roller derby, the best sport on four wheels. No, the best sport ever, full stop.

Annie definitely couldn't leave the match now. Not with Kelsey prancing about, thrusting her hips and sticking her chest out as the cheerleaders danced. Kelsey had made it all too clear she wanted Tyler for herself.

"Come on, Lexie," Annie said. "There's only ten minutes left. And this is for the regional championship. Besides, what kind of person leaves before the end of a match?"

Lexie let out a breath that hung white in front of her mouth. "A cold one? It's got to be below zero."

Annie put her arm around her best friend and gave her shoulders a rub. It *was* pretty cold. In London, where Annie had grown up, it wasn't often this cold. But Annie figured she might as well get used to the weather. She had moved to Liberty Heights, Illinois a few months ago with her dad. Although she missed her mum and England, Liberty Heights had some great things going for it and a little bit of cold wasn't going to send her packing.

Annie kept watching Tyler and the match while trying to

comfort Lexie. "Pretend you're Vincent van Gogh and can't afford to heat your garret, but you're on the verge of finishing your masterpiece."

"No good, I can't feel the pencil to draw any more." Lexie flexed her hand to get the blood flowing again.

Annie tore herself away from the game for just a second to glance at her friend. Lexie's fingers poking out from fingerless gloves did look a bit blue. Lexie was passionate about her art and never missed an opportunity to work on it. *Maybe*, Annie thought, *she'd enjoy the match if she'd give it a chance.*

But Annie wasn't going to say that to her best friend. Lexie and sport were like ice cream and garlic; they just didn't go well together. The last thing Annie wanted was to argue with Lexie.

"Tell you what. Stay with me, just until it finishes, and I'll make you the most gorgeous hot chocolate you've ever had when we get back to Rosie Lee's."

"Fine." Lexie struggled to turn the page of her sketchbook. "But it had better have lots of whipped cream."

"Well, yeah. You know my dad makes it himself." Annie imagined the fresh whipped cream and decided that she might just have to enjoy a gourmet hot chocolate too.

After Annie's mum and dad separated, Dad had decided to return from London to his hometown in Illinois to follow his dream of opening up a British-style café. It was called Rosie Lee's, Cockney rhyming slang for tea. While it had got off to a slow start, business was steady now, especially with the festive season approaching.

It had been a hard choice for Annie to choose which parent she wanted to live with. She had grown up in London and definitely felt British, but Dad pretty much raised her while Mum worked at her law firm. Dad had always been there for Annie and she couldn't imagine life without him, even if it meant leaving the familiarity of England. Still, Annie couldn't help but hope that maybe her parents would get back together one day.

Annie got to her feet as the Panthers tried to score a goal, but before it got to the keeper, Tyler somehow soared several feet into the air to head the ball back to Javier. Great pass!

With five minutes left on the clock, Annie couldn't take her eyes off the pitch. The ball was going back and forth between the teams, but the Stags still held on to their one point lead. If they could keep it up, Annie might be kissing a regional champion tonight! Annie let out an excited high-pitched squeal and Lexie responded with a sound of exasperation.

Annie offered Lexie her scarf, but Lexie shook her head. Poor Lexie. If only she could enjoy the game. There had to be a way to make her feel more connected.

"Did I tell you what the team did to the coach?" Annie smiled at the memory of Tyler telling her the story. "Tyler and Ethan bought a live turkey from a farmer the other day and put it in the coach's front yard. The coach freaked out when he came home. The bird started chasing him and wouldn't let him get in the house. The coach had to call animal control and they spent hours chasing after the bird throughout the neighbourhood." Annie laughed as she imagined the scene.

"Hilarious," Lexie muttered.

"Don't worry, they caught the turkey and brought it to an animal sanctuary."

This time Lexie grunted but didn't look up from her sketch. Maybe it was more than just the cold. Maybe Lexie and her mum were fighting again. Though Annie got along well with Lexie's mum, she knew Mrs Jones wished her unconventional daughter would be more straight-laced. It wasn't fair how parents always wanted their kids to be different than who they were. Annie had the same problem with her mum back in London.

She hugged her legs to her chest and tugged on the hat that covered her long brown hair. OK, maybe it was a bit colder than she'd let on. That was the disadvantage of being so tall (5'11"½) and slim. There was no place to store body heat. Everyone had warned her about the midwestern winters and it was only November. At least there wouldn't be any more soccer games until next autumn.

Annie glanced at the sketchbook again. Instead of complimenting Lexie's artwork, Annie frowned at the sketch. Lexie's gloved hands were covering most of it.

"Hey, what's that?" Annie asked, reaching over for the sketchbook.

Lexie quickly flipped the book over to hide what she had been doing. "Nothing. Just something I messed up on."

Annie didn't know what to say. She'd seen the sketch for the briefest second when Lexie had moved her hands. Still, it was long enough to know what she saw: a soccer player with an uncharacteristically large head, cheesy grin, and a speech bubble that said, "I'm so awesome." It could have been any of the players, but Lexie was too good of an artist not to make him clearly identifiable. Thanks to the exaggerated cheekbones and the perfect hair, Annie recognised him easily: Tyler.

Annie realized that Lexie didn't really like her boyfriend. But then again, Lexie didn't like most jocks and the attention they got. She was resentful that athletics got much more funding than the arts. But getting together with Tyler was one of the best things that had happened to Annie since she moved to the United States. Surely Lexie could make an exception and like this one particular jock.

Annie knew, though, that it wasn't exactly one-sided. Tyler thought Lexie was a bit eccentric (he used the term "weird freaks" to describe Lexie and her friends from manga club). But Tyler read the comics in the newspaper and that was kind of close to the graphic novels Lexie read. They had that in common at least. Annie really liked both of her friends and giving up one for the other wasn't an option. Maybe if they spent more time together, they'd realize how great the other was. They would just have to find a way to get along. Besides, they did have another important thing in common…

Annie.

Read *In a Jam* to find out what Annie does next!

Hooked on roller derby?

Here are three more fast and furious *Roller Girls*
books about Annie and her friends.

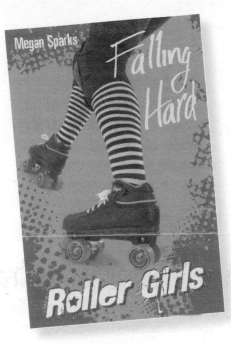

Falling Hard

After Annie Turner's parents split up, she thought moving to the USA with her dad would be an exciting new start. But she's struggling to fit in. For a start, the most popular girl at school hates her! Things finally begin to look up when Annie discovers the wild sport of roller derby and a whole underground scene she'd never even known existed. And then there's Tyler, a green-cyed football player who literally makes Annie want to drool in public…

Is Annie tough enough to make it as a roller girl?

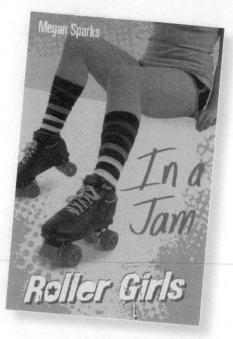

In a Jam

Life couldn't be better for Annie Turner. Not only is she
going out with the dreamiest boy she's ever met, but her
roller derby team is riding high in the league. But OF
COURSE, just when things seem to be working out, it
all starts falling apart. Annie gets left on the bench at a
big bout, her best friend can't stand her boyfriend and
her mum wants her to quit the team!

Will Annie listen to her heart? And what is it saying, anyway?

Boot Camp Blues

Annie Turner is single again and it really kind of sucks. It doesn't help that her ex is now going out with a cheerleader! But she's also confused by her new feelings for skater boy Jesse. They're just friends … aren't they? Meanwhile, Annie and her roller girls are each desperate to make the cut for an all-star team. Tensions run high as the teammates compete against each other for roller glory.

Will the stars in Annie's eyes get in the way of her friendships?

For more exciting books from brilliant
authors, follow the fox!
www.curious-fox.com